full moon *kisses*

ALSO BY ELLEN SCHREIBER

ONCE IN A FULL MOON

MAGIC OF THE MOONLIGHT

VAMPIRE KISSES: THE BEGINNING

VAMPIRE KISSES

VAMPIRE KISSES 2: KISSING COFFINS

VAMPIRE KISSES 3: VAMPIREVILLE

VAMPIRE KISSES 4: DANCE WITH A VAMPIRE

VAMPIRE KISSES 5: THE COFFIN CLUB

VAMPIRE KISSES 6: ROYAL BLOOD

VAMPIRE KISSES 7: LOVE BITES

VAMPIRE KISSES 8: CRYPTIC CRAVINGS

VAMPIRE KISSES 9: IMMORTAL HEARTS

VAMPIRE KISSES: BLOOD RELATIVES

VAMPIRE KISSES: GRAVEYARD GAMES

TEENAGE MERMAID

COMEDY GIRL

ELLEN SCHREIBER

full moon
kisses

a full moon novel

KATHERINE TEGEN BOOKS
An Imprint of HarperCollins Publishers

To my husband, Eddie,
my parents, Gary and Suzie,
and my brothers, Mark and Ben

HarperTeen is an imprint of HarperCollins Publishers.
Katherine Tegen Books is an imprint of HarperCollins Publishers.

Full Moon Kisses

Library of Congress Control Number: 2012949623
ISBN 978-0-06-198653-6 (trade bdg.)

Typography by Amy Ryan
13 14 15 16 17   LP/RRDH   10 9 8 7 6 5 4 3 2 1
❖
First Edition

CONTENTS

1. Haunted Moon   1

2. Lycan Lunch   18

3. Field Trip   25

4. Father Knows Best   48

5. Mr. Worthington   71

6. Doctor's Visit   81

7. Rude Boys   95

8. Girls and Gangs   112

9. Wicked Werewolves   130

10. The Search   137

11. Sisterly Advice   155

12. Canoe Trip   160

13. A Few Good Friends   167

14. The Brave One   175

15. Werewolf Fest   185

16. Moonlight Meeting   199

17. Full Moon Kiss   211

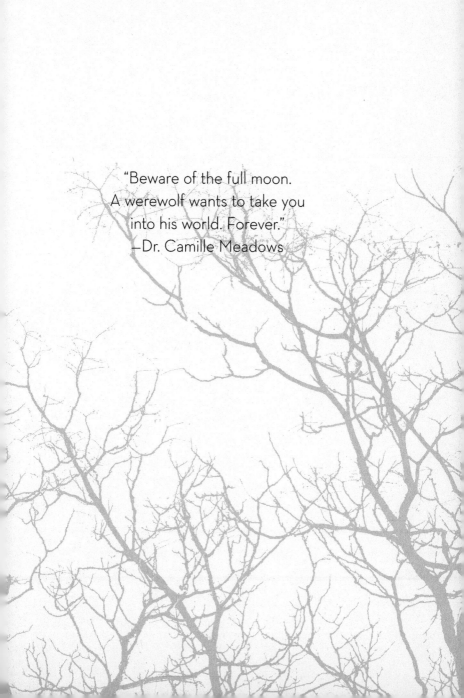

"Beware of the full moon.
A werewolf wants to take you
into his world. Forever."
—Dr. Camille Meadows

ONE

haunted moon

The full moon glowed brightly above me and Brandon, the handsome werewolf I'd fallen in love with, as we stood cuddling, surrounded by a friendly pack of wolves, deep within the wooded area behind his grandparents' home in Legend's Run. I could taste Brandon's lips on mine and feel his powerful strength as he enveloped me in his embrace. His woodsy scent was intoxicating, and his wild, dark hair seduced me like a rock star's. I didn't want our evening together to end, but, unfortunately, I knew it had to. Brandon and I couldn't spend the rest of our lives in the woods away from our families and friends. Or could we?

I had more on my plate than I could handle. I was in love with a lycan, and my former boyfriend, Nash, was now one, too.

"What do you think will happen?" I asked Brandon as I looked up at him. "Now that Nash knows that he's a werewolf, what will he do? What will *we* do?"

Two months ago, Nash had been bitten by a wolf and subsequently, under the full moon, had become a lycan. And just like Brandon, he didn't remember his actions while he was transformed. But unlike Brandon, Nash was aggressive when he turned, and he'd become a threat to me, the town, and himself. I'd discovered that kissing Brandon when he was a werewolf caused him to become aware of his lycan state so that he remembered his actions in his daylight, human hours. And it was important for me and for the sake of others that Nash remember what he was doing—as he was doing it. Also, he was tormented not knowing what was happening to him. I wanted to help him, for his sake as well as mine. The kiss under the full moon was the only remedy, so a few hours ago I'd kissed Nash when he had turned into a werewolf.

Nash was popular and very attractive, and he and I'd been going together on and off before I met Brandon—but something had always been missing between us. And now, of course, I was completely in love with Brandon—in his normal, human form *and* in his werewolf state.

Hair poked out from the top of Brandon's open shirt, and my fingers caressed the top of his normally smooth chest.

"We can't predict everything—nor can we control it," he said, his voice strong. He brushed his hand against my cheek. "We can only control what we do. And that is continue to be together, even under these strange circumstances." Brandon's hair, which hung savagely wild a few inches above his shoulders, flopped over his gray eyes. He drew me into him again with a powerful and reassuring hug. His chest was warm and rugged. I knew he could crush me with his strength, but he was as gentle as he was strong.

I loved Brandon's confidence; I was drawn to that as much as I was to his gorgeous human and now lycan features.

"Could we just stay here forever?" I asked, dreaming.

His wolf fangs poked out from his smile and caught the moonlight. It was as if he was really contemplating his life in werewolf form.

"Do you like being a werewolf?" I pressed.

Brandon didn't respond.

I thought about my feelings regarding his being a werewolf. My life had always been predictable: the same friends, the same school, the same house. But now that I was in love with a werewolf, I didn't know what was happening day to day. On normal days, I had the positive things like my classes, friends, and this new love to juggle. But the addition of Nash and Brandon and their lycan condition made everything that was perfect turn into chaos. I had to admit there was some excitement in not knowing what to expect. It brought out a side of me that I didn't know existed; a spontaneous and adventurous girl was emerging as I experienced things I never had before—walking with wolves in the woods at nightfall, moonlight picnics, kissing werewolves.

I wanted everyone to be happy and to get along, but I wasn't sure how anything could be normal. Now that there were two werewolves in town, I didn't know how any of it would work out. And I wasn't sure that I wanted it to. Brandon had this abnormal condition that he had to deal with every full moon. At those times, he was extraordinary, handsome, and powerful. I couldn't help but see positives of his being a werewolf—it made him stronger and even more heroic.

But for Brandon, it had to be difficult. I could see how awaiting his change, and then transforming, tormented him. It wasn't something that he could control, and it made him different, more so than just being a Westsider among the popular Eastsiders. If people knew about his condition and didn't think it was a joke like they had at the spring dance, it could be life threatening for him. It was unusual, to say the least, and no one would want a werewolf running around their town. But when he was a werewolf there were moments, like now, when he seemed at peace, even seemed to thrive. When we were deep in the woods experiencing nature, away from the hustle and bustle of the rest of the world, with untamed wolves nipping at his heels, he seemed very contented. Just as I found positives when he was in his superhuman form, I wondered if he did as well.

Brandon still didn't respond, and his bright mood seemed to change. "We'd better go," he said. "It is getting late."

After tonight the moon would wane and I'd have to wait another month until I saw Brandon in this lycan form again.

Neither one of us wanted to let the evening end, me holding on to my werewolf for the moments I was able to see him in this form—and though he didn't say it, I sensed he enjoyed getting to explore a more powerful side of himself and to experience nature without the fear that a human might. But the clouds began to join together, covering our unobstructed view of the moon. It was as if the evening sky were telling us, too, that our night together was over, and we'd soon have to face the weeks ahead waiting for the next full moon.

The next day, I met my best friends, Ivy and Abby, at our local coffee shop. We liked to get together to discuss the latest gossip and upcoming events, and the friendly, cozy café offered our favorite drinks and an intimate space to chat. Our coffee hangout had local artists' pictures showcased on the walls, several bean-bag chairs to hang out in, and even stacks of board games and books for patrons to use while they enjoyed yummy caffeinated beverages. Even though I would have loved to get out a game and challenge Ivy and Abby, we always managed to drink and gab our time away and forget about the games. Cool, hip jazz music played as the barista took our orders. It was warm outside and I wasn't in the mood for something hot, so I chose an iced coffee, and we sat at our usual table.

"Isn't it great we all have found true love now?" Abby said.

"Yes, it is," Ivy agreed, "only I wish you would have told

us about Brandon sooner." She looked at me with a little bit of hurt in her eyes.

It was going to be a little while before I would live down not telling them about my romantic relationship with Brandon.

"So we still have a happy sixsome—just a different one than we imagined," Abby said to Ivy.

"Yes," Ivy agreed. "Just as long as you are happy," she said, turning her attention to me. "And you are, aren't you?"

I nodded enthusiastically.

"Then it's settled," Abby said. "We'll have boyfriends for all events and dances for the rest of high school."

"Then it's off to college," Ivy said, grinning.

I returned the smile, but inside I was uncertain that the world they imagined was as easy as the one I would be living in. My friends had their whole lives planned out. Since I'd met Brandon and he became a werewolf, I considered us lucky to get through each day. I fantasized about my future together with Brandon, but college? I hadn't thought that far ahead. He and I had so much to figure out before then, which was mostly what to do about his lycan condition.

"Well, we still have time," I said, thinking.

"Not much," Ivy said, cupping her coffee mug with her hands. "We have to start planning these things well in advance. College is so hard to get into. We can't wait until the last minute."

"She's right," Abby chimed in.

"Have you even talked to Brandon about it?" Ivy asked.

"Uh . . . no," I admitted.

"She's too busy kissing him," Abby said, laughing.

But Ivy turned serious. "It's something you should be talking about," she said in a voice that was similar to "mother-speak." "We need to get all our ducks in a row," she continued.

I had so much to worry about—like Brandon and Nash being werewolves—how could I take on our future plans for college now, too?

"Uh . . . do you think Brandon can afford college?" Ivy asked me gingerly.

I was taken aback by her question. "Why wouldn't he?" I wondered.

"Uh . . . it's just that he's . . ."

"A Westsider?" I asked.

"I didn't mean . . ." she said sheepishly.

Abby rolled her eyes at Ivy.

"I don't see why he couldn't go," I said defensively. "Just because he lives on the other side of town means he doesn't have money?"

"I didn't mean to . . . I was just concerned," Ivy said. "That's all."

"Dylan and I are hoping to get athletic scholarships," Abby said, diverting the topic back to her as she added some sweetener to her drink. "But we have to promise that we all are going to the same university."

"Duh," Ivy said. She lifted her drink for a toast. Abby held up her latte, and I slowly raised mine.

I reluctantly clinked cups with them.

If only life were that easy, I thought.

I couldn't even begin to contemplate going away to college right now. I was thinking about full moons, transformations, and distant howling in the night. How could Brandon go to college as a werewolf? It was hard enough going to high school and dealing with its assorted complications. And even with its issues, high school didn't have night classes or dorm living to deal with. Those would be new challenges he'd have to deal with in a university setting.

My sister, Juliette, was away at college now. Her life was filled with late-night parties, studying and, for some of her classmates, part-time jobs. How was Brandon going to fit into all of that?

"I think Jake could get an athletic scholarship, too," Ivy said. "But I'm not sure what kind I could get."

"You don't need one," Abby said. "Your dad could pay for *all* of us."

Ivy scowled at Abby. "So could yours."

In fact, they both could easily afford college without any outside help. It was my family that would have to take out a loan.

"It's okay, nothing wrong with being rich," Abby said as if she weren't rich, too.

"Well, you have a big, fancy house right next to mine," Ivy argued back.

"Yes, but my dad's still paying alimony for his first wife. We were hoping she'd remarry by now but she never did."

We all pulled a face and laughed.

"What about you?" Ivy asked me. "You could get a scholarship for being a humanitarian. You are so sweet and kind and the only person we know who volunteers because you like to."

"Uh . . . I haven't thought much about it yet."

"But it's not far off. Only a few months until school ends, then it's senior year!" Ivy exclaimed.

She and Abby clinked their coffee cups again.

They turned to me as I stared at my ice cubes.

"What are you so moody about?" Ivy asked. "Is it Brandon? Don't you see a future with him?"

I paused. My heart said yes. But my mind was unsure. Anyway, it wasn't that I couldn't see a future with him—it was that I knew he was unsure about his own future. What was to become of him?

Last month, his scientist father had sent him a possible cure. It was to be taken under a full moon. And Brandon hadn't taken it because he'd shown up at the dance with me—and then, when we found out Nash had turned, too, he wanted to wait so he could protect me if Nash was violent in his werewolf form.

And what did we understand about this cure anyway? What was it made from? We didn't know if it had even been tested on anyone—or anything. If that wasn't bad enough, we only knew that it *might* work, and there was a possibility it could have the opposite of the intended effect and make Brandon a full-time werewolf. Or maybe there was a chance that the antidote wouldn't work at all.

"Maybe we should just think about 'now'?" I suggested. "There is so much for us to enjoy today."

"So true," Abby said. "Like our field trip to the zoo this week . . . Oh, and the Legend's Run Werewolf Festival is only four weeks away!"

"The zoo?" I wondered aloud.

"Yes, don't you remember?" Ivy asked. "Our spring field trip. It's been on the school calendar for a while. Why are you so distracted, Celeste?"

"I didn't even look at the school calendar," I said truthfully. Other than checking the calendar for the date of the next full moon, I'd been so preoccupied that I was lucky to even get my homework completed.

I loved animals and I hadn't been to the zoo in ages. Ivy, Abby, and I mostly hung out at the coffee shop, high school games, and the mall. So I was definitely excited about the trip, hoping it might be a great distraction for Brandon and me.

"And then, the Werewolf Fest," Abby said. "Won't that be fun?"

Every ten years, Legend's Run held a Werewolf Festival to celebrate the myth of the Legend's Run werewolf—which, from recent experience, I knew was more fact than fiction. It was a huge celebration in town with outdoor movies, all the shopkeepers setting up booths, and a werewolf look-alike contest.

I was seven when I attended the fest the last time. My parents took me and my older sister, Juliette, and I remember it like it was yesterday. There were prizes to win and fun things to buy—and a stalking or happy werewolf on every corner. The outdoor venue showed werewolf movies all night long, like the original *Wolf Man* and *The Howling*. But I was older now and I'd be going with my friends and my boyfriend. My parents would probably go together; Juliette would be away at school with her beau of the month.

"Yes," Ivy replied. "A blast."

"Are you guys going to dress up?" Abby asked, blowing on her latte. "The winner of the costume contest gets a hundred dollars."

"Me, dress up as a werewolf?" Ivy asked, cringing. "I don't know. I don't think Jake will think I'm so hot with fur on my face, will he?"

"I'm going to dress as a girl who was attacked by a werewolf," Abby said. "I've got a dress that I'm going to tatter in shreds. I think that's hot. You can use your imagination, too."

"I'm not so clever," Ivy said. "But maybe I could wear something prickly. Would serve Jake right. When he gets that five o'clock shadow, it really hurts. Could be time for payback."

We all laughed.

"I bet you can come up with something really awesome," Abby said to me. "Your Halloween outfit was supercool. Little Red Riding Hood. You could wear that."

"I guess I can," I agreed.

And what is Brandon going to come as? I wondered.

It would be a full moon. I guessed he could come as himself.

Nash had been a prankster in our school for years, so many believed that he and Brandon had pranked the school dance a few days ago—and that they weren't *real* werewolves but fake ones. And no one wanted to admit in the light of day that they weren't in on the joke. Some even still gave Nash high fives as he made his way down the corridors.

I couldn't help but feel uneasy about their lycan situation. We only had a little less than four weeks until the next full moon, and we'd all have to deal with their transformations again. Would we always be able to dismiss these occurrences as a prank? Or would everyone discover the truth?

Nash caught me in the hall on the way to class on Monday. "I need to talk to you," he said urgently. My former boyfriend was always trying to get back together, and I figured this time was no exception. I was reticent to start another quarrel, but he seemed adamant that he speak with me immediately.

"Uh, can't this wait until after school?" I tried as I hurried toward Ivy and Abby, who were already waiting outside our classroom.

"No," he said, taking my arm and leading me into the alcove of the hallway.

I wasn't thrilled to find myself alone with him in the narrow doorway that led to the theater.

Nash appeared harried. His normally neatly styled sandy-blond hair was tousled, and his mood was urgent. "I want to thank you," he said intently. The last time I saw him, his eyes were gray, and he was in werewolf form. I was on the end of his lips, kissing him under the full moon in hopes that his memory would come back to him when he was a lycan.

Nash was dreamy and it was hard not to fall under the spell of his good looks, but I was in love with Brandon. I had to resist.

"For the other night," he began. "I'm really grateful for what you did." His words were as sincere as if he'd been waiting a lifetime to tell me.

"You remember?" I asked. He'd seemed to gain his consciousness that night but I wanted to make sure his memory lasted.

"Everything." He drew in a breath as if he was breathing me in, too.

I nodded, relieved. This meant that the plan Brandon and I made had worked. Nash was now aware that he had been a werewolf. Having him remember was the only way to control how he acted when he transformed. If he knew what was happening, and what he was, it would give him reason to curtail any violent behavior before it was too late.

He gently placed his hand on my shoulder. "That kiss. It meant a lot to me."

"It was the only way—" I said. I didn't want him to think I wanted us to reconnect.

But then his demeanor changed. "I remember transforming," he said in a worried whisper. "Running through the woods. Destroying the baseball shack." Then he grew even more concerned. "Terrorizing you at the lake—and at the Moonlight Dance." His voice began to waver.

Nash was referring to his first transformation, when he chased me through Willow Park, and another when he burst through the doors of our spring dance and almost attacked me.

I hated that he had to go through such an unearthly transformation. Even though we weren't together anymore, I certainly wouldn't wish for him to have to deal with such an unusual issue.

"It's okay." I tried to comfort him. "You were a . . ."

"I didn't mean to do those things," he continued. "Especially to you, of all people."

"Of course you didn't," I assured him.

"But at the time, I wasn't myself. Not like I am now."

"I understand." I tried to convince him. He was under a considerable amount of stress and turmoil—the effects of remembering his actions.

Nash looked at me intently again, this time his eyes full of sorrow. "I'm not sure you do. I'd never dream of hurting you. I hate the thought of making you afraid of me."

"I know."

"But those nights, I was different, Celeste. Everything changed. I changed, my whole world changed. I felt like an animal."

"Well, you kind of were," I said with a slight laugh.

He didn't smile. "But the kiss," he continued. "That was one thing that was the same. You and me, like old times. It meant everything to me that you did that. I'll never forget it."

"I wanted you to remember, to be aware while you were transformed, and that was the only way I knew how to help you. That's all it was. It was like breaking a spell."

"But I was a werewolf!" he whispered vehemently. Then he paused as a few students passed by, clearly out of earshot. He drew in closer. "And you stood there, shaking, and kissed me anyway. You were so brave—even though I've never seen you so frightened."

"I had to. It was the only way to help you," I said again. I couldn't seem to make him understand my motivations. Nash spent his nights in lycan form as if in a dream, without control or awareness of his behavior. Two lives and memories separated by the full moon; now they all were one. Maybe it was harder for him to deal with it now than before he understood.

"And Brandon. I know it just about killed him to see us together," he said, almost gloating.

This time I didn't respond. Then the bell rang. "I should get to class now."

"I don't want you to fear me," he said. "Not under a full moon. Not then—or ever."

What is he going to do now? I wondered. But I didn't have time to find out.

"Celeste? Hurry up!" Ivy called from down the hallway.

"I've got to go—" I started off, but Nash blocked my way.

"One last thing . . ."

"Yes?" I asked quickly.

"I have to fight this. There has to be some way to cure this horrible condition. This can't keep happening to me every full moon. I have games, school. . . . I have a life."

"What can I do?" I asked.

"You are the only one who knows, besides Brandon. But *you* are the only one I can confide in."

I didn't know what to say. I felt flattered that Nash still felt that I was his one true friend. But was I supposed to take on his issues as well as my own and Brandon's? I thought I'd solved that with the moonlight kiss. Of course I wanted to help my friend, but at the moment, I didn't know how to help him any more than I did Brandon.

"Do you think there is some way to fix this?"

"I'm sure there will be." I tried to reassure him, even though I didn't know if there was. I didn't have time to go into Brandon's possible cure. And how could I when there was only enough for one and I didn't even know if it worked?

"You are the only one I can talk to about this. . . ." he lamented. "Am I supposed to tell my parents? Would they even believe me? I've been pranking people for so long, no one will take me seriously. I need to find a remedy. I only have a few weeks until this awful thing will happen again."

"We can talk later," I said.

"This can't wait. I have to speak with Brandon," he said urgently.

"About what? There's enough tension between the two of you already." Now that Nash remembered our kiss, I feared he'd want to confront Brandon about our relationship.

"It's not about you and me," he said. "This is about Brandon and me. I have to do something before anything bad happens, Celeste. I already demolished the shack and threatened you. But we have to find a cure."

Just then the second bell rang.

Ivy and Abby called me again as they slipped into class. "I have to go," I said. "I'll be late."

As I turned away, he stopped me once again. "You are my lifeline," he said genuinely. "Thanks to you, now I remember everything, Celeste. *Everything.*"

I gave him a quick nod, then broke away and hurried off to class to find solace in the company of my friends and a lecture that I was only hoping I could get lost in. I thought I'd remedied our problems with him with the moonlight kiss. But with him wanting me to ensure that he found a cure, it seemed like Brandon and I had to find a cure for all the werewolves in Legend's Run. It was a lot to ask—but maybe I could help. Maybe on the next full moon Brandon and I really needed to test the antidote his father had sent to make sure it worked.

TWO

lycan lunch

After third bell, I caught up to Brandon at his locker. He was grabbing a textbook, and when he spotted me a huge smile came over his face. For a moment I thought he was going to kiss me. But the crowd of students prevented him from displaying his affection and instead he brushed his hand against mine.

"Hey, Celeste," he said.

I knew I had a worried look on my face. I could feel it, my brow wrinkled and my lips tense. I held my notebooks tightly against me as if they were a shield.

"What's wrong?" he said.

"Nash . . ." I said privately. "He wants me to help him find a cure."

I knew it had taken a lot for Brandon to stand by while I kissed another guy—especially when that guy was interested in me—all for the sake of making him deal with being a werewolf. Brandon's selflessness was so dear to me—I cherished it, but I knew that deep down, that act still pained him, as it would me if I were in his situation.

"He feels like I'm the only one he can trust. Who else can he tell? Dylan? Jake? I know it must be lonely for him," I said sympathetically.

"He's going to use this to try to get back with you," he said.

"I don't think so," I said firmly. "I really think he just wants to find a solution. I'd tell you if it were any other way."

Brandon shook his head. "To think your major problem could have been dating a guy from the wrong side of town. Now you have as many headaches as both Nash and I do."

It was so gracious of Brandon to think of what I was going through when he was the one who really had to deal with a life-altering situation. It was only my issue vicariously. "And I think that Nash feels like you two are kindred spirits now, I guess," I said.

"Did you tell him about my father and the serum he sent me?"

"No. I didn't think it was the time, nor my news, to share. Anyway, since you haven't taken it, we don't even know if it works. I didn't want to get his hopes up. Especially since you only have one dose. Should I have told him?"

"No, not yet. I agree, we need to know if it works first. You did the right thing." Brandon embraced me.

We got a few stares, but I didn't care. The insider with the outsider, the Eastsider with the Westsider, the human with the werewolf—none of it mattered. I felt so warm in his arms and comforted by him. It was heaven to be with him, and it was as if just being in his presence—let alone wrapped in his embrace—took all my worries away.

"It's time for lunch," Brandon said, pulling back.

"Who can eat?" I asked wearily. But I knew Brandon must be starving. Since he'd become a werewolf, his appetite had grown to the size of a sumo wrestler's. The smell from the cafeteria wafted through the hallways, and I heard his stomach begin to growl.

Lunch bell should be a happy time, a break to relax, eat, and hang out with my friends and new boyfriend. But I knew we'd be seeing Nash in the cafeteria, and I wasn't sure how he was going to react or what he was going to say after our talk an hour ago. With Brandon by my side, I wasn't sure if it would bring out more of the animal in Nash even in the daylight hours. After all, Brandon was hungrier than normal and could communicate with canines all the time now. I wasn't sure how Nash would behave with me and Brandon sharing a simple lunch at our normal table.

However, as Brandon took my hand and we began to walk through school, I lost track of all things except being in his company. I was in heaven, our fingers entwined and our arms touching as we passed empty classrooms and students milling in the hallways. I'd never felt so alive and at peace at the same time. I'd always been happy, but something had been missing deep down inside my soul—until I met Brandon. I saw how

Abby and Ivy lit up when their boyfriends were around and how they planned their futures together. And now that I'd met Brandon and fallen in love with him, the inner turmoil I'd once felt about my romantic life was replaced with warmth and joy. I couldn't have been happier—except that I now had to deal with the consequences of my boyfriend being a werewolf.

And this was the first time I was taking Brandon to eat lunch with me at our group's table. Before, I'd eaten at his table or by myself, but this time I wanted him to be part of my group, which he should have been long ago. However, I was having second thoughts and wasn't sure if I wanted to take this on after my conversation with Nash. What if he brought it up again somehow? Or tried to make Brandon jealous by saying he needs me, too?

"Should we just eat alone today?" I asked Brandon as we reached the cafeteria. "We could eat near the library instead."

"I'm not afraid of sitting at Nash's table. Are you?"

"No," I said with a sigh. But I was afraid of the awkwardness, of the secrets that I was still keeping from my friends, and that Nash might very well slip and reveal his and Nash's condition.

And who knew? Maybe Nash was so focused on finding a cure—perhaps instead, he was searching for answers in the library—that he wouldn't be eating with us anyway, and I wouldn't have to deal with it today at all.

I squeezed Brandon's hand as we walked through the cafeteria and outside to the patio. My friends were already at our table, and Abby waved us over while Ivy smiled. I loved the outdoors and was happy to have lunch in the open air. The sounds of birds played in my ears and the fresh spring breeze blew through my hair. I would have loved my classes to be outside, too, but I knew that would never happen. This was my time to feel the freedom and invigoration that nature offered.

I walked to our table with Brandon. Ivy and Abby and Jake and Dylan were already eating, but by their polite gestures I knew they were accepting of us. I was just hoping this wasn't a mistake, bringing Brandon here to be taunted by Nash, who watched us as we approached.

I didn't make eye contact with Nash at first as we stood at our empty seats.

"Hi, guys," Abby said. "Sit down. We've been waiting for you."

Nash gave me a quick glare. Then his face brightened. "Yes, we have." My former boyfriend didn't protest.

I'd given him the gift of remembering his lycan nights. Why couldn't that be enough for him?

"Hey, Brandon, why don't you sit over here?" Nash said, scooting over.

We all looked at him oddly. Was it a prank? Was there a tack on the bench or something worse?

But Brandon didn't seem too bothered and sat down next to Nash.

Ivy gasped and Abby giggled under her breath.

"Seems like you have a new friend," Abby said to my former beau.

"Yes," Nash said. "We're going to be great friends. We have so much in common now, right, Brandon?"

It appeared to the others that he was talking about me, but I knew Nash was really referring to fixing their werewolf problem.

Brandon didn't respond and instead squeezed my leg underneath the table.

The two guys opened their bagged lunches. Brandon had five sandwiches, and Nash had four, plus three protein shakes.

"Dude—football tryouts aren't until late summer," Dylan said, surprised at their lunches.

"Gross. How can you eat all that?" Ivy asked.

"It's the spring air—" Nash said. "Makes me feel like an animal. Do you feel like an animal, too, Brandon?"

"What is he talking about?" Ivy whispered to me.

"Oh, nothing. Just a joke between friends," Nash said.

"So, boys, are you excited for the Werewolf Festival?" Abby asked. "It's only a few weeks away!"

"Oh, yeah," Dylan said. "We'll have to get tickets soon."

"The girls and I have already made our plans to dress up for the festival," Abby said proudly. "Will you guys? There's a hundred-dollar prize for the best-looking werewolf."

"That could be me," Nash said.

The girls giggled, but I knew what he was really referring to.

"What about you, Brandon?" Abby asked. "Are you going to dress up?"

Ivy and Abby treated Brandon so nicely, I regretted taking so long to tell them the truth about my love for him. I should have known they would include him, and I still felt guilty for misjudging them. However, their support made our friendship even stronger.

"I guess, if Celeste is."

Brandon appeared pleased with his new set of friends. I knew eating alone at that table for so many months had to have been so lonely. It killed me that he ever had to be there in the first place.

"What are you going to wear?" Nash asked him. "A costume?"

I nudged Brandon's leg under the table.

"He can be the brave huntsman that saves me," I said. "I'm going to come as Red Riding Hood. I still have the costume I wore for Halloween. It will be perfect."

"Or maybe he can be the Big Bad Wolf," Nash said.

"In that case, he might not need a . . ."

I shot Nash a look as if to say, *Stop talking now.*

But he was delighted with his inside jokes. The sad part was that my hero might look more like a werewolf than the attendees wearing their costumes.

THREE

field trip

Legend's Run was a small town spotted with sprawling communities, high-end and strip malls, and tons of chain restaurants. However, to get to more cultural activities, one would have to drive to the big city, which was less than an hour ride from our cozier town. Our neighboring city had sports stadiums, an accredited art museum, and a renowned zoo.

Every year the junior class went on a spring field trip to the zoo. There was a special feeling in the air on Thursday when students at school knew that we would soon embark on a fabulous field trip. With a school outing came freedom— a day clear of pop quizzes, long lectures, and sitting all day indoors. It would be an educational and relaxing time for all of us. And boy, did I need it. It would be great for Brandon and me to walk around the zoo and hang out with our friends.

I was stoked, waiting in line next to Brandon and Ivy to board the buses. Even though I enjoyed school, it was just as much fun to be taken away from it as to be driven to it.

Nash eyed me as I got on the bus with Brandon.

Brandon watched as I slipped into an empty seat, and he sat down next to me and slid his hand over mine. I looked back at our school, where the lower classmen were having a day like any other. I breathed in and sighed, releasing the tension, as if I were a yoga instructor.

As we pulled away from campus, there was a lot of hooting and hollering from the back of the bus, and Nash and some of his jock friends had to be scolded by the bus driver.

I breathed easier as we made our way out of Legend's Run High and onto the country roads. The open windows blew the breeze through my hair, and the warm sun seemed to kiss my cheeks. We passed fields of wheat and corn, grazing cattle and beautiful horses, spring flowers and trees in bloom. Yards were decorated with colorful tulips, daffodils, and potted plants and adorned with American flags and plastic geese. Birds were singing, and I felt exhilarated. I glanced over to my friends to see how they were enjoying our outing only to find them listening to their MP3 players and playing with their phones. Most students weren't even looking out the window. I felt sad, as they were missing out on the very things we were supposed to be enjoying and experiencing by being on a field trip.

I glanced at Brandon from time to time, and he seemed just as pleased as I was to get a break from school and take in the fresh air and sounds and sights of nature. However, our bus soon passed a strip mall and then turned onto the highway. It was exciting to get the chance to travel with Brandon on a field trip, and we intertwined our fingers as we passed corporate offices, car dealerships, and chain restaurants.

After a long drive on the highway, we passed through part of the city with its high-rise buildings and then saw signs for the zoo. It wasn't too much longer before we saw cars lined up on the street and the entrance to the zoo. Our bus pulled into the lot, and the boys in the back row started making ridiculous chimplike noises. This time, the bus driver ignored them as she was moments from parking.

One by one, we all exited the bus and made our way to the zoo's entrance, where one teacher did a head count while a volunteer from the zoo handed us each a map and a checklist of many of the animals at the zoo, with a blank area underneath where we had to write our observations about them. We were instructed to visit every major animal habitat and to meet at the zoo's entrance by two o'clock.

Ivy immediately veered off from our group and headed for the gift shop. Abby had to drag her out, appeasing her with the promise we'd have a chance to shop before we boarded the bus again to leave.

Ivy and Abby caught up to Dylan, Jake, and Nash and then joined Brandon and me and we all headed out for the exhibits. We girls were first to arrive at the cat house. The exhibit was both indoor and outdoor, and we proceeded to watch the Bengal tigers as they were resting in the sun. As the guys caught up to us, the tigers began to stir in their enclosure. For a few moments, the big cats sniffed the air and several of them began to stretch. Then a few of them squinted and perked up their ears. Several slowly rose and began to pace back and forth in front of their younger cubs. As we watched them, they continued to pace and we took a few notes before we thought about heading to the next enclosure. The adult tigers started to growl, and we were taken with their roars. Their growls grew louder. Then we realized the tigers were staring straight at Nash and Brandon.

"That's weird," Ivy said. "They don't like you guys."

Brandon backed away, but Nash stayed and waved his hands wildly. The tigers were still on their rocks and cave-like formations. One tiger stayed with the young, but another began to walk off the rocks and through the pond that separated the visitor's fence and the tiger's habitat. It was creeping over toward Nash.

"Can't you read?" Abby scolded him. She pointed to a sign that warned against taunting the animals.

The tiger was in its pen and at least fifty feet away. But it wasn't stopping or turning its direction. It was heading straight for us. And even though we were safely protected by a wire fence, it was creeping closer. We could see its eyes as, now not more than twenty feet away, it waded step-by-step, through the pond toward us. I wasn't calmed by the steel fencing, and I moved away, as did Ivy and Abby.

"You might want to stop," Jake warned Nash. "I don't think that's smart."

Nash immediately stopped waving his arms. But the tiger didn't pause.

Nash was as frightened as we were by the imposing tiger and retreated from the fence.

The tiger drew closer still and locked eyes with Nash. Then it growled. We could feel his breath and massive roar, and we girls screamed. Ivy and Abby ran a few feet back but Nash, Brandon, and I remained frozen.

"Let's get out of here," Nash said. "I never liked tigers anyway."

The tiger brushed against the fence, and other onlookers were also startled that it had approached us so closely.

We scurried away and as I glanced back, I still saw the tiger watching us until we were out of view.

We all laughed awkwardly and shook our heads at the weird incident. I was wondering whether others might have thought it to be bizarre—or if they were just passing it off as Nash taunting the animals.

"Scaredy-cats," Jake said to Abby, Ivy, and me as we made our way to the next habitat.

"I thought it was going to kill us," Abby said.

"I could have saved you," Jake said. "With my bare hands."

"Are you kidding? You were the first one to run away," Dylan needled.

"Hey, it was coming after Nash, not me," he said. "And it seemed to have its sights on Brandon, too."

"Even with a fence between us," Ivy said, "I was still freaking."

"I think it wanted to eat Nash for lunch," Dylan teased as he put his arm around Abby's shoulder.

We all laughed again, and Brandon grabbed my hand and my friends took comfort in their boyfriends' arms. Nash cracked a few jokes, but I could tell he was still a bit shaken by the tiger's threatening advance toward him.

We decided to visit the primates next. As we all arrived at their habitat, we looked at our checklist. Ivy was first to spot the species of primates on our list, and we quickly checked it off—chimpanzees.

The primates were behind glass and had trees and metal bars to climb and swing on.

One was looking straight at us as if he was checking us out, gawking at him.

"He's so cute," Ivy said. "I want to take him home."

"Until he rips your arm off," Jake replied.

"He wouldn't do that," she went on. "He's too cute. Look at that face."

"Aren't you already dating a chimpanzee?" Nash jabbed Jake in the side.

The chimpanzees were sweet looking, but I had seen

news stories that they could be violent.

After a few moments of viewing them, they began to walk around and swing on the bars. They started to call out in high-pitched voices: "Ooh, ooh, ooh."

A mother chimp held her baby and made her way behind a tree as if she was protecting the small primate from something. As the other chimps still called out, a third one came up to the glass near where Nash and Brandon were standing. Suddenly it began banging on the glass. We all pulled back and quickly walked away.

"Still want to take him home?" Jake asked Ivy.

Ivy grimaced at her boyfriend.

"He's still better behaved than you are," Dylan teased.

Brandon looked at me curiously. "I've never seen a chimp do that," he whispered to me. "It was like it was staring right at me."

"And Nash," I whispered.

I glanced over at Nash to see his reaction. He was walking toward the next exhibit but was glaring at the chimpanzee. "Maybe they aren't feeding their animals today," he said to me.

We moved over to the black-handed spider monkey habitat and checked off the correct species.

They were in an outdoor enclosed pen with a huge wooden structure that they could climb on. We all observed the animals so we could fill in the rest of the information required on our sheet.

"Those are so cute! I want one," Abby said, pointing to a few monkeys who were high atop the structure.

The spider monkeys were sitting on the top picking at each other. As we took notes, they began racing around frantically and shouting out in repetitive and high-pitched calls.

They continued to race around frantically until we decided to move to the next habitat.

A gorilla was sitting on the grass, eating a piece of bamboo, fifty yards away from us behind its glass enclosure. It wasn't long before it took notice of us. It stood up and glared at Brandon, then Nash.

"This is weird," Ivy said. "It's like the gorilla is looking right at us."

The gorilla growled. Dylan began to grumble back at it.

"Don't do that," Abby said, slapping him on the shoulder. "Have some respect for the animals."

But the gorilla continued to stare and growl. Suddenly it began to beat his chest. All the spectators pointed at the large mammal and started taking pictures.

But we were disturbed by its behavior, especially Brandon. This animal, like the others, seemed to once again focus on our group.

"I think we should go," he whispered to me.

"Let's get out of here," Ivy demanded. She dragged Abby away from the crowd.

We raced back down the hill, passing a few other habitats. The animals began to pace—and many of them cried out:

tweets from the birds, *hurmpt*s from the elephants, roars from the lions. When we reached the bottom of the hill, we tried to slough off the odd behavior of the animals.

"Maybe it's because it's spring," Abby said, "but these animals are crazy."

"I agree," Ivy said.

Then Jake tickled her. "They aren't the only ones who have spring fever," he teased.

"This is really weird," Abby stated. "I've never been to a zoo where the animals acted this way."

"I haven't, either," Dylan said. "It is freaky. But maybe Ivy's right about the spring weather. Brings out the animal in all of us."

I agreed that we all needed a break from the animal action. A few yards ahead of us was the zoo's kiddie train. It was big enough for adults to ride in next to a child, but it was obviously meant for kids and their parents. Each carriage was brightly painted with a different animal on it, and the engine was candy-apple red. Nash insisted we ride the train to the opposite side of the zoo.

We girls resisted at first, but Dylan and Jake hopped on and waved their girlfriends over. We tried our best to squeeze into the carriages together and keep our limbs from hanging out. Ivy, Abby, and I giggled as the train took us slowly through the park and stopped at the foot of the hill that led to the giraffe exhibit. We hopped out and giggled some more as we made our way up the hill.

Heidi Rosen and a few of her friends were already at the entrance. "This smells," she said. "I can't go in there."

"I wonder what the giraffe thinks of her," Abby said snidely. Ivy and I chuckled together.

"I think I'll stay out here," Brandon said.

"Afraid of a giraffe?" Nash said. "What are you, chicken?"

No, werewolf, I wanted to say. Didn't he realize that the animals were bothered by their presence? It was as if it wasn't even registering to Nash how the animals had been responding to them.

"I'll wait out here with Brandon," I said.

"Need some alone time?" Ivy teased as she and the rest of the gang proceeded into the indoor giraffe exhibit.

Brandon and I headed back down the hill and hung out on a picnic bench a few yards away from the Mexican wolf exhibit. We heard a few howls from the wolf enclosure. A woman was holding a small child as he stood on the lowest rung of a wooden fence around its perimeter. He leaned over the edge to look down at the animals.

"It is bizarre, but the animals must be sensing something about you and Nash," I said, draping my leg over his.

"You think so, too?" he asked.

"Uh . . . yes. It seems pretty obvious to me."

"Do you think the others notice that, too? That it's Nash and me?"

"Well, that one time Nash was tormenting the tiger, so

perhaps they'll chalk that one up to him. But every habitat? It is really weird."

"Maybe the school bringing two werewolves to a zoo wasn't such a good idea for an educational field trip."

"Well, I think we are learning. A lot," I said truthfully. "Just as much about the animals as about you and Nash. You really have side effects beyond just the full moon. It is in you all the time—being a . . ."

"I know. They sense it obviously," he said. "But what can I do? Stay inside twenty-four seven? It's frustrating, really," he said.

I rubbed his arm—one that was now smooth but would be lined with a fine layer of hair and have muscles like a tri-athlete's in a few weeks.

"Well, maybe we can hang here for a while," I encouraged. "Let us rest—and the animals, too. Let's just enjoy the time together and having a day off from school. It is really beautiful here, with the pretty trees and flowers. And it's not too often I get to see wild animals this close up."

"Yes," he said. "It was kind of cool. But I like it better here, where it's just the two of us." He put his arm around me and drew me close. His brilliant blue eyes glistened like the peacock that was waddling away from us a few feet away. Brandon leaned in to kiss me.

Just then we heard a scream.

The small boy was gone, and the mother was straining to look down over the wooden fence.

"Help! He's fallen into the enclosure!" she screamed. "Please help me! Someone please—he's fallen!" She began pointing and looking around wildly, trying to signal someone to help her.

Without hesitating, Brandon raced over to the exhibit. I tried to run after him, but I couldn't keep up with him. Before I knew it, he leaped over the fence. I saw his hands holding on to the bottom rail for a moment before they disappeared.

I covered my mouth in disbelief. I was afraid for his life.

"What are you doing?" a man yelled to Brandon. "You'll get killed!"

I was afraid not only that Brandon would be attacked but that he would be injured in falling to the bottom of the enclosure.

"Brandon—what are you doing?" I shouted. I raced over to the fence and looked down at Brandon and the boy.

The boy was lying on a grassy area about fifteen feet below us, just underneath the fence where he had fallen. Brandon was standing between him and a pack of wolves about twenty feet away from him. The wolves huddled together as if they were wondering if they were going to be attacked by the intruders. Brandon stepped between the boy and the wolf pack, staring at them. I wasn't sure if the wolves would attack, but they were snarling as if they might.

Suddenly Ivy, Jake, and Nash were standing behind me.

"What's going on?" Ivy shrieked as she ran up to me. "What is Brandon doing in the wolf cage?" she asked, terrified.

Brandon continued to stare at the wolves, and they backed up slowly. Eventually they relaxed and knelt as if obeying a command.

Brandon remained in front of the child, who was stirring awake, while keeping the restrained wolves at bay. Several zookeepers hurried into the enclosure with long, metal prods and tranquilizer guns. But the wolves were already calm and lying down. One zookeeper quickly led Brandon and the boy out of the enclosure.

Nash was as white as a ghost. "I can't believe what just happened. That could have been me," he said. "Perhaps it should have been. . . ."

"You could have fallen into the enclosure?" Jake asked.

But I knew what Nash meant. However, he didn't jump into the enclosure. In fact, he didn't even move—until now.

We hurried to that side of the enclosure and waited impatiently for Brandon and the boy to come out.

A few moments later a side door opened, and the boy, along with a zookeeper and Brandon, appeared.

The mother raced to her son and held him, clinging to him with all her might, as a few paramedics and zookeepers came to check the boy out. He had several cuts and bruises but, apart from that and being traumatized, he seemed all right.

The boy began to cry as his mother fussed over him.

"You saved my son's life," she cried when she saw Brandon. "You are a hero."

Brandon blushed.

"I don't know how to thank you. You just stood there in front of those wolves. I can't imagine what you were thinking . . . but I am so happy you did. I don't know how I'll ever be able to repay you."

"You don't have to," Brandon said. "I'm just happy he's all right."

"Tommy, this young man helped you. Can you say thank you?"

The boy was visibly shaken and clung to his mother. He was too upset and shy to speak.

"It's okay," Brandon said.

"Thank you so much again," the mother gushed.

Brandon smiled as the paramedics attended to the boy, and we began to walk away from the wolf habitat.

"I should have filmed it!" Jake said. "It would have gone viral."

I held on to Brandon, who was breathing heavily. Brandon acted calm, as if he didn't recognize his own heroic actions.

"So what are we going to see now?" he asked.

"How about we have lunch?" Ivy asked. "My heart is pounding, and I need to sit down."

"Me, too," I said.

I squeezed Brandon's hand tightly as we walked over to the outdoor café, sat at the picnic tables, and began ordering.

Abby and Dylan finally caught up with us and ordered, too. "So what was all the big excitement we saw over by the wolf habitat?" Abby asked.

"Didn't you hear?" Jake said to Dylan. "Brandon saved a kid!"

"He was going to be attacked by a pack of wolves," Ivy said.

"They weren't going to attack," Brandon said.

"Uh, tell that to the kid's mom!" Ivy said.

My friends were very taken with Brandon's heroics and kept complimenting him.

Nash appeared jealous, as the attention from his friends and schoolmates was centered on Brandon.

A few moments later, the waitress returned with our meals.

As Nash and Brandon ate several sandwiches, my friends continued to gloat over his bravery.

"You can build up an appetite being a superhero," Abby said about Brandon's eating.

Even Jake and Dylan were impressed by the handsome Westsider. "You really have guts," Dylan said. "You wouldn't catch me dead in a wolf enclosure."

"Ha! You'd probably *be* dead if you jumped in there! Brandon must be a wolf whisperer," Jake joked.

"Yes, it was amazing what you did," Abby said.

Brandon was too close to the event to bask in the glory of being a hero. I think he was still stunned at what had happened. Or maybe it was like nothing at all to him. That he jumped over the fence and saved the boy was like eating lunch in the cafeteria. Something normal and everyday. He did seem overwhelmed with the attention, however.

Brandon and Nash finished their meals quickly.

"We'll get your dessert for you," Ivy said. "You relax." She got up from the table.

"Uh . . . that's okay." He tried to stop them. "I can get it."

But Abby waved him off. "You sit. Let someone do something for you now."

"Yeah," Jake said. "We need you to catch your breath in case a kid falls into the lion's den next."

Jake and Dylan followed the girls and met them at the ice-cream stand.

"That is so nice of them," Brandon said sincerely. He was so touched by my friends' generosity. "But really, I can get my dessert. I'm all right."

"I know, but it might be a good idea for you to unwind for a minute." I caressed his back and smoothed out his shirt, which had bunched up a little when he was jumping into the enclosure.

"Are you going to get mine, too?" I heard Nash ask after Ivy.

"When you save a kid's life, maybe," Abby shot back. They were already ordering Brandon's sundae.

Nash muttered under his breath and turned back to us. He saw me smoothing out Brandon's shirt. I could see a loneliness in his eyes. He was a werewolf, too. But he wasn't the one to face the wolves, and I think he felt like the odd lycan out.

As our friends were taking care of our desserts, we were

approached by a few zoo administrators.

"I'm Kevin," a lean man in a khaki zoo uniform said. "Are you the guy who jumped into the wolf habitat?"

I was eager to share Brandon's heroism, and I beamed proudly. But he inched back as if unsettled. "Uh . . . only if I'm not in trouble."

"Yes, normally that would be a criminal act. But in this case, we can't really cite you since you saved a boy—and the wolves as well."

Now Brandon was the one beaming. He wasn't going to be in trouble, and he felt good about bringing a peaceful end to the incident.

"I'll need to get some information from you." Kevin sat down at our table with the other administrator, and I sat close as Brandon answered questions for the zoo's incident report.

After a few minutes, Brandon had completed the man's queries.

"I think that's all for now," Kevin said. "We'll call you if we have anything further."

"All right," Brandon agreed.

"But one more thing," Kevin said. "Can I ask what made you do that? Just jump into the enclosure? Wolves don't normally confront people. But in this situation? Who knows."

"I don't know. I didn't think about why," Brandon answered. "Just that I had to."

Kevin shook his head. "But to have just stood there so calmly in front of a pack of wolves. Most people won't stand in front of a pack of barking dogs. And you couldn't have known what would happen to the kid—or you."

"He knows more than you think," I said to Kevin.

"Well, we know he's brave and agile. That's for sure," Kevin said.

I smiled proudly at the compliments about my boyfriend.

Kevin gathered his things and rose. "We are happy to have had you here. And hopefully your next visit will be a lot less eventful." He handed Brandon a book of free tickets to the zoo.

He shook Brandon's hand and left just as our friends came back to our tables with ice cream.

A few other students started coming into the outdoor café and had noticed the zoo administrator with us. They kept peering over and began whispering. As more students came in and joined them, they began to gossip and all began eyeing us. I assumed that word was spreading about Brandon's heroic deeds in the wolf enclosure.

Nash came back with a triple cone—twice as much ice cream as Dylan and Jake had. Ivy handed Brandon a banana split sundae.

"We know how you like to eat," she remarked.

"Thank you so much," he said. "I really appreciate it."

Nash and Brandon tore into their supersized desserts. We all watched in awe.

"Abby was right. Being a hero must build up an appetite," Ivy said to Brandon.

"And doing nothing must build up yours," Jake teased Nash.

Nash scowled. It was a strong jab, and I think it really hurt him.

"That's okay," Brandon said. "He wasn't in the area when it happened. Otherwise he would have done the same thing."

Nash brightened. He sat up straight and a smile came over his face. He was really pleased with Brandon's coming to his defense.

We continued to eat, and I felt exhilarated sitting next to a once-again hero.

When we all finished and were discarding our trash, I wondered if it was such a good idea to go back through the park. We'd only completed half of our required checklist, but I didn't see how we'd be able to hang out in front of each exhibit without Brandon and Nash disturbing the animals with their presence.

Brandon must have felt the same thing as he sidled up to me when we left the café. "Maybe we shouldn't go right up to the habitats," he said. "We can get an idea of what the animals are doing from a distance. Don't you think?"

I nodded. "Yes, I think it might be best to give them— and you—some distance."

"Well, we have half of the park left," Jake said to our group. "Mainly sea animals, so I hope no one falls into the shark pool. That would be gruesome."

"Do you know how to swim, Brandon?" Dylan teased.

Brandon laughed off the joke and seemed to be in good spirits, but I know he was concerned about the animals' reactions. He'd drawn enough attention for one morning, and we didn't want any more coming our way. It was hard enough to explain the earlier events, and I wasn't sure how much longer we could keep hiding it.

On our way to the rest of the park, we walked by the area that led to the cat house attractions; we could hear the roar of a lion. I wasn't sure if it was disturbed by Brandon's and Nash's presence or if it was giving my boyfriend kudos for his bravery.

When we reached the sign for the manatees, Brandon and I slowed down.

"I think we'll hang back," I said to the others.

"You're not afraid of wolves but you are of manatees?" Jake prodded.

"We're not afraid," I retorted. "Just want to see other parts of the zoo, too."

"Yeah, me, too," Nash said. "I'll hang with them." He stuck next to Brandon and me, and we accepted his company. I felt for him. He was going through the same thing Brandon was going through.

"That's okay," Ivy said. "We'll catch up to you."

"All right," Abby said. "But these guys are acting so weird today."

"We'll be able to see them from here," I said.

"Do you have telescopic vision, too?" Dylan teased.

"Leave them alone," Ivy scolded. She linked arms with Jake and pulled him toward the manatee attraction.

"I thought I only had to worry about the full moon," Nash said to me when the others were out of earshot. "I wasn't expecting this, too."

"Neither was I," I said.

Brandon was silent.

"But you were?" Nash asked Brandon.

Brandon shrugged his shoulders.

"You know. Tell me. It's happened to you longer."

"I've sensed things during the day, too, since this has happened. Yes."

"Like the time at school when the wolves appeared outside our classroom?" Nash said, piecing the events together.

"Yes," Brandon said.

"And the time you saved me from the wolf attack?" Nash continued.

Brandon nodded.

"But elephants and lions?" Nash asked with a laugh.

"I haven't come across them in the woods," Brandon said lightly.

"Animals sense other animals," I added.

"I'm an animal?" Nash said to me. His voice was angry, as if I had hurt him.

"I didn't mean—" I began.

"But, yes," Brandon interjected, putting his hand on my shoulder. "They sense us."

Nash sat on the bench. He was deflated by the reality of his lycan situation. "I just want to be normal. Be myself again. That's all."

I sat by him. "I know. This is hard on us all."

"But you aren't the one changing," he challenged me.

"You are right. It just hurts me to see you both deal with this."

"I'm sorry," Nash said. "I shouldn't have snapped at you. We really need to come up with a plan," he continued. "I can't deal with this every day. We have to get this thing fixed."

"I know," I said.

Just then our friends caught up to us. Nash, Brandon, and I chose to hang back several yards away from the rest of the exhibits, viewing the animals and making our notes from afar. It seemed to work, and the animals behaved normally. We didn't have much time for private conversation as Ivy and Abby returned quickly each time as if they felt like they were missing something by not hanging back with us. I held hands with Brandon as we walked through the park, checking the remaining animals off our list. Before I knew it, it was almost two o'clock, time to meet our bus. We headed to the front of the park and as we waited by the entrance for the other students, Ivy, Abby, and I ducked into the gift shop.

Abby and I got a few zoo key-chain keepsakes for us and our beaux.

Ivy came out with a plush wolf and handed it to Brandon.

"Here," she said. "Something to remember today by."

"Thanks, Ivy," Brandon said. "That's really nice of you." He seemed truly touched by my best friend's generosity, and so was I.

Nash scowled again and quickly boarded the bus.

"Maybe next time we should stick with the botanical gardens," Dylan said.

"But Nash might frighten the Venus flytraps," Jake teased.

The pair laughed as we all settled in our seats, and our teacher took another head count.

"Students," the teacher said in a serious voice, "I'm sure I don't have to tell you that no one is ever encouraged to engage in dangerous activities on school-sponsored field trips. And today could have become a very tragic day because of the potentially dangerous actions of one of our students," she admonished. "But that said, I'm rather proud to say that we have a hero on this bus, and his name is Brandon Maddox."

Cheers and clapping erupted from the students on board. Brandon blushed from all the attention as Nash gave him a knowing glance.

father knows best

When we walked through the hallways before first bell the next day, I noticed students eyeing Brandon as if he were the school quarterback.

"Word must be spreading about the zoo," I said. "You are getting stares."

As we approached a few upperclassmen, one of the seniors caught sight of Brandon.

"Hey, dude—" he said, high-fiving my boyfriend as they passed.

Brandon turned to me as shocked as I was.

When we got to class, I heard Abby talking to the girl seated next to her.

"It's like he's communicating with them," Abby said.

"He did that same stare when a wolf pack showed up at school," Ivy said.

"We saw that happen," Abby said.

"We were right there," Ivy went on.

"There he is!" Abby said, now noticing us.

Brandon turned red. He sat in his chair in the back of the room and busied himself with his notebooks.

Later in the day, on our way to lunch, a few girls from the Eastside were hanging around us as if they wanted to talk to him.

One girl pushed the other into Brandon.

"Excuse me," she said, embarrassed while her awaiting friends giggled. She gazed up at Brandon with crush-girl eyes. Then she scurried back to her friends.

"You touched him," one girl said as they continued to giggle. "Now you can't wash that arm for a week."

They all squealed to themselves and made their way to class.

"So now you have groupies," I said. I did think it was sweet that the girls thought Brandon was a dreamboat—just like I had always thought he was.

Brandon didn't boast, but the students hung on his every word as if they were meeting a celebrity.

Following that, a few freshman boys approached Brandon.

"Can I take a picture with you?" one asked.

Brandon was taken aback by the question. "Uh, yeah, I guess."

The boy quickly stood at his side and made a peace-sign gesture as his friend snapped a picture of them together.

"Now it's my turn," the other said.

"Okay . . ." Brandon did the same. I watched as my boyfriend was being treated like he was on the red carpet of a movie premiere.

When we finally got to lunch, the rest of our group was already eating.

Two freshmen came up to Brandon. "We heard what you did. That was major cool. Could you sign this?"

He handed Brandon a notebook.

Brandon quickly scribbled his name.

"This is getting crazy," Brandon said. "I'm not a hero."

"Uh, yes, you are," Ivy said.

"Well, I just want to be like everyone else," Brandon said.

"Then don't jump in cages and talk to wolves," Jake teased.

When another kid came up, Dylan rolled his eyes. "Dude—he's eating," Dylan said. "Give the man some space. He'll be signing autographs in the theater during fifth bell."

"Okay, I'll see you then." The boy seemed pleased and went back to his table, and Dylan and Jake laughed.

Nash couldn't help but scowl. He tried to hide his disdain for the attention Brandon was receiving by bringing up other subjects.

"We have some tough games coming up. We're going to have to really hustle to beat Huntington Saturday."

But Ivy and Abby weren't keen to talk about games they weren't playing.

"The Werewolf Fest is only three weeks away," Abby said. "I can't wait to go!"

"Me, too," Ivy said. "It's going to be so much fun!"

Nash turned to my friends. "What's so great about werewolves?" he asked.

"Well, it seems like you like them," Ivy shot back. "You and Brandon were the ones who dressed up like them at the dance."

"Oh yeah," he said. "But that wasn't so much fun after all."

"Well, you had us all fooled. We thought for a while you might be the Legend's Run werewolf reincarnated," Jake said.

We all laughed. *If they only knew,* I thought. *If they only knew.*

I was leaving my last class and heading to my locker when I saw Heidi Rosen talking to Brandon by his. I quickly hurried over, as she was twisting her hair in major flirt mode. She had her hand on his forearm and then, when she caught sight of me, she smiled sweetly at him and turned and walked away.

"What was Heidi doing talking to you?" I asked.

"She said she heard about what happened yesterday at the zoo. And that she only wished she had been there to see it."

"Weird. She never talks to us."

"Then she invited me to her party this weekend."

I was shocked and hurt. A streak of jealousy scorched through my veins. I didn't like another girl inviting my boyfriend to her party when she was clearly not inviting me, too.

"Are you going to go?" I asked nervously.

"Uh . . . no. I told her I had plans."

I breathed a sigh of relief.

"It's really strange. Not only has becoming a lycan changed my behavior but the behavior of the other kids, too."

"I know. But you deserve fame and fortune."

"I don't," he said. "Not really. Anyone would have done the same thing in my situation."

"No," I said, "not anyone."

Brandon couldn't be just like anyone else now that he was a werewolf. And because he used his strength and powers for the good of others instead of becoming a monster like Nash had only made him that much dearer to me.

"I don't want this attention. It's not normal," he said. "But I do like helping people." Brandon was clearly astonished that saving the boy at the zoo had brought him sudden fame. So it wasn't just the full moon that changed his life—everything was different now.

"You can be a hero, too, as a human," I said. "You saved me from the wolves before you were . . ."

"Bitten."

"And if you hadn't, none of this would have happened." I still felt guilty for being the cause of his torment. If I'd heeded Dr. Meadows's warning, Brandon wouldn't have to deal with this condition.

"But then you might not be standing here," he said. "Don't worry." He took my hand. "I don't regret it for a minute."

I squeezed his hand back.

"It's only three weeks to the next full moon," I assured him. "You'll take the serum and all this might go away."

"I'll take the serum," he continued. "And then we'll know. Right?"

"And maybe we can get more for Nash."

"Always thinking of others," he said.

I shrugged my shoulders.

"But I agree. We need to help him be cured just as much as we need to make sure I am."

I put my arm around his waist and leaned into him. He was as giving as I'd want any boyfriend to be, as good a person as he was a sexy werewolf. I knew I'd miss the side of Brandon that came out under the full moon, but it was more important for him to lead a normal life than it was for me to get a werewolf's kiss.

The following Monday, Brandon caught up to me before school. "My father is coming again," he said. "This Friday."

"That is great news," I said. "I bet you'll be glad to see him."

"I will be. But . . ."

"But what?"

"I think he's coming because I didn't take the serum during the last full moon. He's on his way to New York for a meeting but is stopping here first. He doesn't understand why I didn't take the medicine then."

"Well, you had good reason. We were trying to help Nash remember, and we needed you to be in werewolf form. And it's less than three weeks to the next full moon. Let him know you'll take it then."

"I will. But I kind of feel bad. He made this for me so quickly, and I didn't use it."

"He'll understand."

"I'm not so sure. He doesn't like it when I don't do what he says."

"No parent does," I said.

"But since he is coming, I'll talk to him about making some more serum for Nash."

Brandon had told me a few days ago that he would ask his dad for more serum, but hearing him say it again—when his father was coming into town—made it really hit home. Maybe we really could help Nash after all. "You would do that for him? You are amazing." I was so pleased that Brandon saw the urgency in the situation and wanted to help Nash again. "It's so generous of you. He doesn't have anyone helping him out."

"Except you," he said.

"I don't feel like I'm much help. Besides, you'd be the one really helping him. And your father."

"I understand what he's going through. He really wants a chance to be normal again. I know he wants it as badly as I do, if not more."

"You don't want it as much as Nash does?" I pressed him.

This time he shrugged his shoulders. "Being able to

communicate with wolves has its advantages."

I was excited that he finally admitted to me a part of what he liked about being a lycan.

"But there are just as many downsides," he said. "I don't know if it's worth it."

"Well, regardless, you'll always be my alpha male."

Nash found me taking my study hall in the library as I was trying to catch up on some of my homework. Studying and my lessons were taking a backseat to all the chaos that was going on around me. Luckily I managed to stay focused in class and keep up with my lessons as much as I could so I hadn't fallen too far behind. I knew my grades needed to remain high as these last two years of school were so important for my entrance into college.

He sat down beside me with some books in tow: *Witches and Werewolves* and *Supernatural Creatures and Their Heritage*.

"That's not your usual reading," I commented. "I'd expect you to be reading *Sports Illustrated*."

"I'm trying to find some way to fix this. The next full moon is only a few weeks away," he whispered, setting the books down on the table.

He was dreading his impending transformation. I could see it in his eyes. They were intense and focused on finding answers.

"Is Brandon trying to get some answers, too?" he asked.

"Yes, he's trying," I said.

"My parents are getting suspicious. My dad says I eat like an elephant, and my mom says I'm eating her out of house and home."

I nodded. "That is happening to Brandon, too."

"And I'm starting to run faster at practice and hit farther than I have before."

"Wow," I said, "you must like that."

"I do. I want to be great. But is hitting home runs worth what I have to go through once a month? The coach thinks I'm juicing," he said. "I could get kicked off the team. Yes, I want to be fast and strong, but not like this. Besides, I can't be a major league player and not be able to play during a full moon because I'm hiding in the woods like a dog."

Nash was tense, and he brushed his hand through his hair anxiously. I felt for him and really wanted to see his pain and stress go away.

He opened one of the books. "I'm hoping there is something in here that can help. I've searched the internet, but nothing has helped me figure this out. I ran and ran to purge my body of this strength and energy, but I didn't even get tired. I just wound up feeling more energized."

"Have you gone to a doctor?" I asked.

"Are you crazy? They'd lock me up. I don't want to be in a funny farm. I'd rather hide in the woods."

I shook my head, almost in despair.

"What is Brandon doing—besides saving kids? I bet he likes this, doesn't he?"

"Why would you say such a thing?"

"C'mon, you can tell me. It's obvious. He can be a hero."

"He's not like that at all."

"Aww . . . he likes this stuff. I can see it. Charming the wolves and getting all this attention. No one knew who he was a few weeks ago—except for you."

"How can you be so callous?" I asked. "If anyone would understand, I'd think it would be you. This has been hell for him, too."

He nodded his head. "You're right. My moods are so erratic. You have to take what I say with a grain of salt. I don't always feel like myself, you know?"

"I know—this is really frustrating for you both."

"So has Brandon found anything worth trying?" he asked.

I wanted to tell him so badly about Brandon's father and the possible cure, but I couldn't. It was privileged information, and it wasn't my news to tell. I could only assure Nash that I was here to help and anything that I could do, I would.

"Nothing that's certain yet. If we do find something that works—you'll be the first to know."

"The full moon is coming. Less than three weeks away. I can't go through this again, Celeste."

I sat in the library with him as he checked through the books for ideas. Once again I was distracted from my homework, busy dealing with the effects of being friends with the new generation of Legend's Run's werewolves.

* * *

A few days passed and I was looking forward to Dr. Maddox's arrival on Friday, hoping he could help Brandon. Since Dr. Maddox was going to be coming to town on a late flight, Brandon invited me over to his house for dinner and to wait for his father. Brandon's grandparents were dining out with another couple, so we'd have the place to ourselves.

Brandon and I had a cozy meal together in the kitchen.

"It's like our own home," I said, checking on cookies I'd placed in the oven. He drew me in and pulled some cookie dough off my fingers. Then he ate the cookie dough.

"Yum," he said. He leaned into me and kissed me. I hugged him and patted him with an oven mitt I had on one hand.

"It would be cool to have our own place someday," he said suddenly.

"You think so?" I asked.

"Yes," he said.

I was so touched that Brandon was thinking about the future—our future.

"Ivy and Abby were talking about college and how we all should go to the same university," I said.

"I hadn't thought about that."

"College?"

"Ivy and Abby," he said. "But that's flattering that they'd like to include me."

"I think you are growing on them. Finding Abby's dog.

Saving a little boy's life. What's not to like about you?"

"The fact that I'm a werewolf," he said. Suddenly his mood changed.

"But we're trying to fix that."

"I know. On one hand, I want to take the serum and get it over with—see if it really works. On the other hand, I dread it. If it doesn't work—"

"We don't have to think of that now. Let's plan on it working."

He laid his hand on top of mine. "I still feel guilty about not taking it last full moon. My dad made this cure for me, and I didn't take it. I'm sure he's really upset."

"I'm sure once you explain, he'll understand. He's coming here tonight to help. And besides, he's your father. You must miss him. It will be great for you to have him here with you."

"I do. He's a great guy—a great dad. I just know how he looked at me the last time he was here. With fear in his eyes. He's afraid of me—his only son."

"He's not afraid anymore," I said. "He is coming back."

"I'm not so sure. It's not natural to have a son who is a werewolf."

"Well, we are working on that, aren't we?"

"Yes, but mostly he is. And I'm the one who resisted his help."

"But there is another full moon coming soon. Don't beat yourself up. You can take it then."

"You are really something," he said. "Most girls I've met are only interested in shopping and partying. You are so understanding. Most girls would run from a werewolf, not date one."

"Well, how can I resist one as cute as you?" I asked coyly.

"I've been dying to do this all day." He sat at the table and pulled me onto his lap and we kissed.

Then we cleared our dishes and put them in the dishwasher.

I imagined for a moment that this was our home. Brandon and me living in the country. A house with character and dogs barking in the backyard, a flower garden, and a wooded area behind the house like Brandon had now. And what if he couldn't change back to normal and he was this way always? Wouldn't it be good for those times when it was a full moon to live in an out-of-the-way spot with a lot of land and a small forest behind the house to run alongside wolves without neighbors knowing? It might be possible to live our lives that way, if we had to. And if we had to, I was up for the challenge.

The doorbell rang, yanking me out of my fantasy and back into reality.

Brandon headed into the front room, and I followed. He opened the door, and Dr. Maddox stood there with a warm smile on his face. He embraced his son.

"Great to see you, Brandon," he said, patting him on the back as they hugged.

"You, too, Dad," Brandon replied.

"Hi, Celeste," Brandon's father said to me.

"Hi, Dr. Maddox," I said.

"Wow, something smells delicious," he remarked.

"Celeste just baked chocolate-chip cookies," Brandon said. "Would you like some?"

"I bet you are hungry from traveling," I said. "We have leftovers from dinner, too. We could heat them up for you."

"No, thank you—but those cookies—that will be great."

I went into the kitchen while the two Maddox men reunited.

I came back into the family room with a full plate of cookies and handed Dr. Maddox a small plate and a napkin.

"Thank you," he said, settling in on the sofa. He took a cookie and bit into it. He grinned, delighted. "These are delicious," he said between chewing. "You are quite the cook."

"It's just from a package," I admitted.

"Well, I'm still very impressed," he said.

Brandon scooted over, and I sat next to him on the love seat.

"So how have you been?" Brandon's father asked. "You sure look good."

"I feel okay," Brandon said.

"Celeste seems to be taking good care of you," he remarked.

"She is," Brandon said.

"But how is everything else? Do you still have the lycan symptoms under a full moon?"

"If you mean 'turning into a werewolf' are lycan symptoms?" Brandon joked. "Then, yes."

Dr. Maddox didn't laugh.

"How are you feeling on a daily basis?"

"Hungry. I'm always hungry. I can see in the dark, and I feel compelled to sleep outside, even though I don't."

"So your daily symptoms are getting stronger?"

"I guess you could say that."

"He can communicate with wolves," I added proudly.

"Really?" Dr. Maddox asked.

"Yes," I said. "And other canines. He's very powerful. He saved a boy at the zoo the other day."

"Interesting," Dr. Maddox said. He put down his empty plate and pulled out his phone. He made a few notes on it. "What happened exactly, Brandon?"

"I don't know . . . I just heard a scream, and then I sensed something—wolves in the distance being threatened. I didn't have much time to think. Before I knew it, I was in an enclosure at the zoo staring at a pack of wolves. There was a boy lying on the grassy embankment—he was hurt and unconscious. I wasn't sure about his injuries, but I didn't want the wolves to attack him—nor did I want the boy to be afraid if he woke up. I let the wolves know that they weren't threatened."

"How did you do that?" he asked incredulously.

"Uh . . . I guess telepathically."

"So it is still happening," his father went on.

"I didn't take the serum. I told you."

"I know. But I thought your symptoms might wane. The restless nights and the like. But I didn't realize you had other abilities, like communicating with wolves. How do you do that?"

"I don't know. I can't explain it. I just make eye contact with them, like I would a human. Only I can sense how they feel and what they are thinking. And somehow they know what I'm thinking, too."

"And they listen," I chimed in. "He's the alpha male in the pack," I told Dr. Maddox proudly.

"This is so interesting. I can't believe it. If you weren't telling me—if you weren't my son, I wouldn't believe it."

"I wish it were all a prank," Brandon said.

"I think we'll have to run some tests. I have to see this and document it."

This made me think of Dr. Meadows and her request, which had alarmed me. She wanted to film Brandon's transformation. But Dr. Maddox was a scientist and Brandon's father. He didn't want to exploit his son for his own gain.

"I was hoping you would have taken the serum and have been back to normal. But since you haven't, I think we need to talk."

"Yes?" Brandon asked.

"I want to know why you haven't taken it," Dr. Maddox said, sitting up. "I thought you would have on the last full moon. That's why I'm here. I wanted to know why and make sure you were okay."

"We think there is another werewolf," Brandon confessed. "In fact, we know there is one."

"You have to be kidding," his father said.

"I'm not," Brandon replied.

"Who is this person?" his father wondered.

"Another guy at school. Nash, Celeste's old boyfriend."

"You seem to have quite a history with werewolves," his father remarked.

We all half chuckled, relieving some of the tension.

"So I wanted to wait," Brandon said. "To make sure he didn't harm Celeste."

"But don't you think you can be yourself and handle these situations?" Brandon's father asked.

"Of course . . . but it does help to be strong," Brandon replied. "And with my communication abilities, I thought I stood a better chance at controlling Nash's werewolf behavior."

"At some point, you have to be yourself and do what is best for you," Dr. Maddox said firmly.

"Maybe this is me," Brandon responded sullenly. "I can't be cured and then have Celeste in harm's way with another werewolf."

"Well, maybe you can," he tried to assure Brandon.

"Yes," he said. "I guess I could. I just was thinking I'd be stronger if I . . . Look, he was also bitten. I saw it happen. I tried to stop it, but I only got there in time for us to stop the wolf before Nash was killed."

"Brandon saved his life," I interjected proudly. "Just like he saved the boy at the zoo. And he saved me when I was lost in the woods. Brandon has been like a superhero in this town."

Brandon's father tapped him on the knee. "You are terrific," he said. "All the problems you are going through, and you have the wherewithal to use your condition to help others. I am truly proud of you."

Brandon's cheeks flushed red. I know he wouldn't admit that getting props from his father meant a lot to him, but he couldn't hide his proud expression.

"And there's something else, Dad," Brandon said. "Now Nash is looking to be cured as well. I want to know, can we give him some of the serum?"

"I made that serum for you. I want you to be normal. Then we can go about seeking cures for your friends. What you have is only enough for one dose. And that dose is for you to take. And if you take the serum, you can prove its effectiveness. Then I can go and make another dose. But for now—I can't give out medication to a minor without considering many legal issues. You understand that, right?"

"I understand. But can't you make more?" Brandon asked.

"I did the best I could in the short time I had to create a possible antidote. It's made from wolf DNA and human DNA. There was no one to test it on, I'm afraid. Just a few mice."

"Werewolf mice?" Brandon asked with a laugh.

"Creepy," I said, imagining their appearance.

"I injected five lab mice with wolf DNA and saliva from a rabid wolf. I used intense reflected light to simulate moonlight and manipulated the magnetic field around their cage to re-create the full moon's gravitational effects on the earth. Within a few minutes, the mice began to grow canine fur. Their muscles also grew stronger and they were much faster than normal. A few days later, I injected the serum, which contained particles of moondust I got from a scientist at NASA. Nothing happened. But when I injected it after their hair was turned under the moonlight, the antidote worked on four of them. They turned back into normal mice."

"But what about the fifth one?" Brandon asked.

"He still continued to grow canine fur."

"That's what I'm afraid of," Brandon said.

"It was only one in five. The odds are in your favor. It isn't likely that you'll stay a werewolf full-time."

"Isn't likely?" Brandon asked, rising. "One in five? What if I'm the fifth one?"

"What choice do we have?" his father asked, rising, too. "Do you want to remain in this condition forever? Eating like an animal during the day, talking to wolves, and then under a full moon turning into one? At least I am giving you a chance to be cured. It's better than what we are facing now."

Brandon turned to me. He knew what he had to do—for himself and for Nash.

"You are my son," Dr. Maddox said in a comforting

voice. "I want you to be able to live a normal life."

Brandon was tormented by his condition and by the decisions he had to make. He didn't want to argue with his father, but he also didn't want to feel compelled to take it knowing there were risks. I could sense that he was thinking about that one little mouse that didn't return to normal.

"What would you do?" Brandon finally asked him.

"I'd take the serum," his father said adamantly. "As soon as the sun sets and the full moon rises." He hugged Brandon tightly.

When he finally let go, Dr. Maddox said, "I'm so tired. I'd better be off to catch some shut-eye. We'll talk more in the morning. I think I'll be able to convince you when I'm rested. Good night, Brandon. Good night, Celeste." He picked up the plate of cookies and walked upstairs.

The following day, I came back to meet Brandon at his house. His father had plans to run some experiments, and Brandon wanted me to be there with them. He said he thought maybe if I was there his father wouldn't "go all medieval on him," as he put it. We only had two weeks until the full moon, and Brandon would be taking the antidote.

Apollo, the husky, was shut inside the main house while we were in the backyard next to the garden.

"Can you call Apollo out here?" his father asked.

"I could do that before." Brandon cupped his mouth and yelled, "Apollo!"

The dog ran to the window and barked.

Dr. Maddox wasn't pleased with his son's humor. "I mean with your mind," he chided. "I just want to test out what you've told me about your abilities as a werewolf."

"Fine." Brandon headed inside and opened the door and let Apollo out. The dog scampered and raced through the garden and backyard, chasing a bird.

"Calm him down," his dad challenged. "Without calling him."

Brandon rolled his eyes, like any normal teen, but then relaxed. When the busy, playful dog caught sight of him, Brandon glared at his pet. Apollo immediately stopped running and walked over to Brandon. Once at Brandon's feet, he knelt down and then fully reclined.

"That was amazing," his father said. He looked thoughtful for a moment. "And can you tell me what kind of animals are in the vicinity?"

Brandon sighed, then reluctantly gazed around. He listened for a minute and then took in a deep breath.

"A hawk is flying this way from due south. Three sparrows are in those two trees. A family of deer is searching for food alongside that hill." Brandon pointed to an area, but I couldn't see anything through the thick brush.

Brandon's father took out his binoculars. He pointed them to the trees and then deep into the woods. "Those are sparrows. And I can see those deer now, too."

A moment later a hawk flew overhead.

Even I was impressed with Brandon's senses.

Finally, after Brandon's father had documented several of his son's unusual powers, it was time for the older Maddox to have dinner with his parents.

"Will you be staying for dinner?" his father asked.

"I have to go home," I said. "I have a major exam tomorrow, and I still need to study."

"Well, it was great seeing you," Dr. Maddox said. "I'll be leaving tomorrow."

"So soon?"

"I'm stopping in New York, then it's back to Geneva. Next time, I hope to stay longer. Maybe for good."

"That would be wonderful," I said.

"But in the meantime, I'm counting on you both to take care of things while I'm away. You have to promise me, Brandon; that serum is for you."

"But what if it doesn't work?" Brandon asked.

"Then we'll go to plan B and fix it then. But at least we'll know."

"I guess. . . ."

"I need you to be convinced. I know this must be hard for you. I'm counting on you to help yourself this time."

Brandon managed a smile.

"And I'm looking to you, Celeste," Dr. Maddox continued. "You will be my eyes and ears. I'm hoping he will take that serum at the next full moon."

"I understand," I said.

I wasn't sure what to do when the full moon hit—to insist

that Brandon take the serum or not—but I knew it was ulti-
mately his decision and I'd be right by his side.

"I know this isn't ideal, me being half a world away from
you," Dr. Maddox went on. "You're in high school, with so
many things happening to you. I'm missing it. You are growing up without me."

"I'm not," Brandon said. "You are right here with me—I
have your serum."

I thought Brandon might have been convinced now to
take the antidote and try it out—if not for himself, for his
father and Nash.

mr. worthington

Brandon had nearly two weeks to wait before he could take the serum and discover how it would affect him. Never mind it could possibly turn him into a werewolf full-time; what if it didn't work at all? What did we know about the serum anyway? Even with Dr. Maddox's reassurance, the anxiety of the unknown was palpable to us both.

And how was I supposed to make sure that Brandon was the one who took it first? It really wasn't my decision, and I felt that Brandon might not want to be cured as much as Nash. But I'd made a promise, and I'd have to keep it.

I tried to hide my anxiety the next day by hanging out with Brandon at his house. But as soon as my mind became unfocused, that was the first thing my thoughts went back to.

Nash sent me texts about how he needed me to help

find him a cure—that he was feeling more agitated with the impending full moon. Brandon was obviously anxious, too, chopping wood that didn't need to be chopped and building things in his backyard that didn't need to be built. In his spare moments, I saw his mind wander, and I knew what it was contemplating: a life forever as a werewolf.

To ease our minds, I thought it might be a good idea to get insight on their lycan plight by getting more information on the whole Legend's Run folklore from the only living resource we knew—ninety-year-old Mr. Worthington. Brandon and I hadn't been to visit him in a few weeks, and I thought he might be happy to have us. And I decided bringing Nash along might help us all.

Later that day, I called Nash and convinced him to meet Brandon and me in the parking lot outside the Pine Tree Village Retirement Community. Nash knew that I had been volunteering here for some time, but when we were dating he always had an excuse not to join me. I think he felt awkward around elderly people—maybe he didn't know how to speak to them or felt sorry for them because they seemed lonely. To me, they were like anyone else, just older. And their stories and lives were that much richer for their years of experience.

I headed in first, with Brandon following me and Nash last in our pack. Brandon stood beside me, and Nash hung back in the foyer while I asked the receptionist for Mr. Worthington. Usually the friendly senior citizen was out in the lobby making small talk or taking a quick nap, but this time he wasn't in sight.

I tried not to worry—but I only felt good when I saw him well, at his age. Every time I didn't see him made me afraid I'd never see him again.

However, my concern eased as the receptionist assured me that he was just finishing a group activity. We could smell chicken baking in the kitchens. Dinner came early at Pine Tree Village.

"I'm getting hungry," Brandon said.

"I'm getting sick," Nash said. "I'd hate to live here."

"Shh!" I said. "You're being rude."

"Where is the old man?" Nash said. "I think I've aged a few years already waiting for him."

Nash's impatience was one of the reasons I didn't totally click with him. I knew he was only hiding his fear—in this case, fear of becoming old and being alone. But Brandon was naturally caring and nurturing. He took care of his grandparents and seemed really pleased when he met Mr. Worthington and found out he was his maternal great-grandfather.

Nash was texting when Mr. Worthington came out from the dining room and into the lobby. The chipper senior citizen was pleasantly surprised to see me and my entourage.

Mr. Worthington was wearing a brown cardigan and khakis. He walked slowly toward us.

"Hello, Celeste, it is wonderful to see you."

"We just stopped by to say hello," I said.

Mr. Worthington extended his hand to my boyfriend. "Brandon," he said. "It's good to see you again."

"And this is our friend, Nash," I said, introducing them.

"It's nice to meet you," Mr. Worthington said. "You can call me Charles."

Nash extended his hand. "I'm pleased to meet you, too."

"Your boyfriends seem to be multiplying," Mr. Worthington said to me with a wink.

I blushed and tried to cover my embarrassment with a soft giggle.

"What brings you here?" Mr. Worthington finally asked.

"We'd like to know more about the Legend's Run werewolf," I replied.

"Great news," he said. Mr. Worthington was always eager to have an audience, and talking about the Legend's Run werewolf was one of his favorite subjects.

"Come, sit down." Mr. Worthington waited while I sat on the sofa. Then Brandon sat next to me while Nash and Mr. Worthington took their places in paisley-patterned chairs.

"What would you like to know?" Mr. Worthington asked.

"We've heard about the Legend's Run werewolf," I began. "But we only know about the one werewolf."

"Yes?" he asked eagerly.

"In the story you told us last time, a man was bitten by him," I continued. "We'd like to know if there is another werewolf. Another bloodline?"

"I'm not sure I know what you mean," Mr. Worthington said. "Bloodline?"

"You told us that your great-grandfather Worthington was rumored to have bitten another man," I reminded him. "That means that maybe there was another werewolf bloodline that carried the curse."

"Oh, yes . . ." Mr. Worthington said. "That is, if you believe in such things. Do you?"

We all nodded in agreement.

Mr. Worthington perked up, pleased with his captive audience.

"My family was very close with another family. The Hamiltons."

Nash, Brandon, and I sat up as if a ghost had just stepped in the room.

"Did I say something wrong?" Mr. Worthington asked, concerned.

"No," I replied. "In fact, you said something right. Please, go on."

"My family—our family—" he said, referring to Brandon, "settled in Legend's Run at the same time as the Hamiltons did. Competition immediately came between the two families. Legend has it that it was over a girl." Then he paused. "Isn't it always? Great wars are started that way."

Mr. Worthington looked at us and gave us a laugh. Nash and Brandon chuckled back politely. I don't think either one of them cared for the joke.

"The Hamiltons were the ones who tried the most to banish my great-grandfather from town," he continued. "It was said that Joseph Hamilton was hoping he could gain control of my grandfather's wealth and the love of his wife."

"Ooh," I said. "It sounds scandalous."

"You might say that," he went on. "But the story goes that it was the night of a full moon when Joseph Hamilton was on his way to confront my great-grandfather in the forest and met a half man, half wolf. It was said townsfolk heard his cries for miles. He didn't return that night. The next day a group of hunters discovered him lying in the woods, violently attacked and left for dead. They returned him to his family, who nursed his wounds. But during the following nights he began behaving strangely. Fierce howling came from his house at moonlight. The daylight showed his home had been ransacked, as if by a wild animal. His wife and children, fearing for their lives, fled. Townsfolk believed he'd come down with a fever, and this was what caused his strange behavior. Those few who believed in the lore of the werewolf swore otherwise. The two men were forced to live out their lives as lonely and haunted creatures of the night."

"Wow . . ." I said.

Brandon shook his head in awe.

"That's it?" Nash asked.

"What did you want to hear?" Mr. Worthington wondered.

"That they all live happily ever after," Nash said, sitting up.

"Isn't it more exciting and mysterious this way?" Mr. Worthington asked.

"No," Nash said. "It's depressing and tragic."

"That's how most werewolf stories are. That's what makes them exciting."

"I don't like that kind of excitement," Nash said.

"It's just legend," Mr. Worthington said. "Folklore that's repeated through time. Just like ghost stories told around a campfire."

"But you believe it, don't you?" I asked Mr. Worthington.

"It doesn't make sense—my great-grandfather was a werewolf?" he asked. "As a boy it always frightened me, and I surely believed it. However, as I grew older I dismissed it, like you grow out of believing in the tooth fairy. But I've always liked to tell the story."

"But what if it isn't just a story?" Nash asked. "What if it really happened and it keeps repeating itself through future generations?"

"You believe it then?" Mr. Worthington asked eagerly. "Then you believe in werewolves. . . . Have you ever met one?"

"Yes," Nash said. "And so have you. In fact, you are talking to one."

Brandon and I were shocked by Nash's declaration. Mr. Worthington stared at my former boyfriend skeptically and then changed his expression. He grinned and began to chuckle.

"This has been so much fun, talking with you," he said. "Celeste has such comical friends. It gives a little liveliness to this place."

"But there has to be more to the story," Nash urged. "Did they find a cure?"

Mr. Worthington thought for a moment. "Not according to legend."

"Perhaps they did and you just don't remember."

"A cure was never part of the story I heard growing up."

"Then the story is tragic," Nash said.

"Yes, it is. But only if you believe it."

"I believe it. And I don't want my story to be tragic, too. My name is Nash *Hamilton*. And the dude that your great-grandfather bit was one of my ancestors."

Mr. Worthington was quite shocked and didn't seem to know what to make of Nash's second declaration.

"Calm down, Nash," I said.

"Yes, let's keep this between us." Brandon spoke in a low but forceful voice.

"I can't hide this anymore," Nash continued. "This is what's going to happen to me? Banishment to the woods? Are you kidding?"

"What is he talking about, Celeste?" Mr. Worthington asked. "I thought your friend was joking. Why is he so upset?"

Nash rose. "This isn't what we came here for. We came here for answers."

A few passing residents gawked at us, wondering what all the commotion was about.

"Answers to what?" Mr. Worthington asked.

"Chill out," Brandon scolded Nash. "I think it's time we leave."

"Yes, Nash," I quietly chided. "You are upsetting Mr. Worthington. And the rest of the residents."

Mr. Worthington rose. "I'm fine," he said. He looked at Nash. "What answers were you looking for?" he asked.

Nash's anger and disappointment turned to sorrow. He placed his hand on Mr. Worthington's shoulder. "A cure for the common werewolf," he said, half laughing.

"There is always a cure for whatever ails you—" Mr. Worthington said. "You just have to look inside yourself for the answer. It is closer than you think."

Nash seemed soothed by Mr. Worthington's comforting words. He shook the elderly man's hand and said good-bye to Brandon and me.

I apologized to Mr. Worthington as Nash left the building.

"Why would he be upset?" he asked, worried. "It's only a story. Nothing more."

"He takes things very personally," I said.

"And what about you, Brandon?" Mr. Worthington asked. "Do you believe that your friend is a werewolf because he is a Hamilton descendant? Is that why you all came here?"

We were taken aback by his questions, and Brandon stumbled for an answer.

"Uh . . . well—"

"I was just joking with you," he said. "You kids take everything so seriously." He patted Brandon on his shoulder. "It's spring. Go out there. Have some fun. And don't let her get too close to that other fellow," he said. "I can tell he's a real wolf."

And with that, a nurse came over to Mr. Worthington and told us it was time for his music activity.

Brandon and I left, distracted by Mr. Worthington's tragic story and his message about Nash. Maybe we'd have to figure out what to make of it and hope that this new generation of werewolves wouldn't have to live out their lives deep in the woods in isolation.

"This makes me feel even stronger that I should take the serum as soon as I can," Brandon said as Nash drove off.

"Really?" I asked.

"The Legend's Run werewolf didn't have a cure. I might have one. It would be wrong not to try it—and since my father won't let me use it for Nash, I'll have to be the one to try it. We can't spend our lives banished to the woods—with no life and no family."

I squeezed his hand reassuringly as we got into his Jeep. I stared out the window as we left the retirement home behind us and thought about the words of wisdom from a man who was helping us far more than he would ever know.

doctor's visit

The next day, Nash seemed distracted in class, and at lunch he didn't make much eye contact. He was a bit moody and perhaps even depressed. As his friend, I didn't like to see him this way. His classwork and attention seemed to suffer. And I knew why—he was consumed by the impending full moon and its upcoming effects on him.

I couldn't blame him. I felt awful for Brandon and for him. If he couldn't talk to anyone about it but me, I knew it was eating away at him. His animal instinct must have been getting stronger since the full moon was a little less than two weeks away.

"Nash has got to be on 'roids." I overheard Dylan telling Jake outside the gymnasium. "Did you see him hit? Every time it's a home run. He's good, but not that good."

"It is odd," Jake said. "But wouldn't he tell us if he was juicing?"

"You'd think so."

"Well, maybe he's just hitting better this season than last," Jake went on. "He wouldn't jeopardize his future."

The following day, after class, Nash found me alone at my locker. "I want you to take me to that psychic," Nash said. "She might know what will happen to me."

"Dr. Meadows?" I asked, surprised.

"Yes. I need to see her. Immediately."

"What, right now?"

"Yes."

"But I have plans with Brandon."

"You always have plans with Brandon. I have to speak with this woman now."

"So go. No one's holding you back."

"I need *you* to go with me. I need to find a cure—and soon. Maybe she can help."

I'd feel odd taking Nash to the modern-day fortune-teller. Every time I'd gone with someone else who wanted to consult Dr. Meadows, it was her advice to *me* that shook me up.

"I'm sure you can handle this yourself," I said. "She won't bite."

However, Nash didn't like my joke and scowled. "I need you," he said sincerely. "I can't do this alone. Please, Celeste. Just this once?"

There was a little part of me that still got a thrill that Nash needed me. Not on the grand scale of true love but as a friend who needed a friend. I always like helping people, and it made me feel good that out of all the people in Nash's life, he still thought of me as the one closest to him.

"Besides, if I find out something, we may be able to help Brandon, too." Nash was totally genuine in his comment, and I was touched that he was thoughtful enough to help Brandon.

"Okay," I finally said. For once, Nash was putting someone besides himself first, and I was moved that he was changing for the better.

"And this time, just you and me," he told me. "If we find out anything, you can share it with him."

I agreed. Though the idea of going back to Dr. Meadows made me nervous, I hoped that maybe she could make us all feel better for a change.

Before I headed out of school, I found Brandon by his locker. I was enamored at seeing Brandon; his brilliant blue eyes radiated through me. And I was so excited at being able to be in his presence every chance I got. I wasn't too happy to let one of those chances slip away, but I knew I had to do it for a friend.

"I have a favor to ask," I said in my sweetest voice.

"Sure. What's up?" His dark hair hung down over his brow.

"Well, Nash wants to go to Dr. Meadows to find out if she knows of a cure and if he'll ever be cured or not."

"He wants to go to Dr. Meadows?" he asked.

I nodded.

"Is he going to tell her he's a werewolf?" he whispered.

"No . . . I don't think so. He just wants her to give him advice."

"So why does he need to go to Dr. Meadows? Why not go to a therapist or a real doctor?"

"I don't know . . . I guess because he's afraid they'll tell him he's crazy. And since Dr. Meadows gives readings, I think that's what he's looking for. Some sort of guidance."

"And Dr. Meadows can tell him?" he asked as if I were as crazy as Nash.

"I don't know," I said, shaking my head. "She'll tell him something. If you give her money, she gives you a fortune."

"What does she know?"

In fact she knew a lot. "I don't have to remind you, she was dead-on about the snowstorm, the wolves, and you saving me," referring to the time Brandon rescued me from the threat of a pack of wolves.

"I still think it's just coincidence," he said. "Or too much reading into what she said."

"Nash is just looking for answers—for someone to help him. He's alone, like you were, too."

Brandon's expression changed. I knew he was sympathetic to Nash's plight. Brandon was alone when he first transformed into a werewolf and now he at least had someone to share his experiences with—even if it was Nash.

"Fine, we'll go."

"Well, there's more to the favor," I began.

Brandon appeared skeptical. "He wants me to pay for it, too?" he joked.

"He only wants me to go with him," I said.

"Alone? Just the two of you?"

"Yes."

"Why can't he go with Dylan or Jake?"

"Because they don't know he's a werewolf. They still believe the event at the Moonlight Dance was a prank. And we really don't need them getting involved, do we?"

"Of course he wants you to go. Can't you see? It's just a ploy to be alone with you."

"I don't think it is. This time I really think he just wants answers—not to date me. Besides, we're taking separate cars. It won't take long, and I'll meet you right afterward. I promise nothing will happen. I'll just go to Penny for Your Thoughts and back."

Normally, possessiveness wasn't something I'd be attracted to in a boyfriend. But I could understand Brandon's concern—Nash was my former boyfriend and kept trying to get back together with me. I'd be skeptical, too, if the situation were reversed.

"I watched you kiss him. Isn't that enough?" Brandon asked.

And there was that, too. Brandon had been more than understanding.

"Yes, it was," I said. "But this isn't about his feelings for me at all. It's about him. He's so frightened now. He wasn't like you when you first went through this. He's afraid."

"You don't think I was?" he asked. "That I am?"

"Of course, I didn't mean that. I just meant that you are so brave. Nash appears brave, but—"

"I don't think anyone wants to be a werewolf," Brandon said emphatically.

Brandon was right. Because he had been so courageous, I hadn't taken into consideration that it was still hard on him.

"Okay, I won't go," I said. "He can figure it out on his own."

It was obvious Brandon didn't want me to go. But I think he also didn't want to forbid me to go and now his jealousy turned to guilt.

"Fine. Go," he said. "Just as long as you don't kiss him again."

"I won't even hug him," I agreed, and gave my boyfriend a warm embrace instead.

I followed Nash's BMW in my car through the Westside and parked in front of Penny for Your Thoughts. It was strange hanging out with him in what he always referred to as the wrong side of town. But he seemed to be more preoccupied with his mission than his surroundings.

"Thanks again," he said sincerely when we met at the door.

Colorful interplanetary mobiles and dream catchers hung brightly, and metaphysical books filled the shop's window.

"I can't believe I'm doing this," he said, looking at the display. "But I have no other choice. I hear she's been right about you guys."

"She has," I said, wishing she hadn't been.

He opened the door for me, and the wind chimes echoed throughout the store.

Nash glanced around, then headed straight for the register. He was bent on getting his reading done.

When no one appeared, he was impatient. "Where is she?" he asked.

"Maybe she's with a client," I replied. "Would you like to leave?"

"No," he said. "I'm here to get the answers I didn't get at that old-folks home."

"Don't call it that," I said.

He was fidgety and tapped his fingers on the counter. When she still didn't appear, he went to look at some of the books on the supernatural and paranormal. "These were the same ones at the library," he said, holding up *Witches and Werewolves*. He sighed with discontent when he didn't find any new information.

A few moments later, Dr. Meadows came out from the back room.

She seemed surprised and delighted to find me waiting.

"Hello, Celeste," she said joyfully. "It's great to see you. Have you come again for another reading?"

"We're not here for me," I said. "My friend wants a reading."

Nash hurried over to the counter.

"Friend?" she asked quizzically as if she was attempting to read our relationship.

"Yes," I said. "Nash is quite excited."

She seemed even more surprised to hear that Nash was the one making an appointment with her.

"Well, it's nice to meet you, Nash," she said, her glittery lashes twinkling.

"You, too," he replied.

"Come on back," she said eagerly. She gestured toward the reading room in the rear of her store.

I followed Dr. Meadows, with Nash close behind.

"Is this your first reading?" she asked him.

"Yes," he said as he entered the New Age room. "And you come highly recommended."

I believed now more than most. Everything she predicted had happened, and that was why I didn't want to come there. I wanted free will—and I didn't want her scaring me with her predictions.

"You're not going to put a hex or anything on me, are you?" Nash said, sitting at the reading table.

"I don't do that. I'm a reader. I can help guide your future."

"That's exactly what I want," he said, relieved.

"Is there something specific you want to know about?" she asked him.

"Yes," he said. Nash became very serious. "I have this, uh . . . condition . . . and I want to know if there is a cure," he said cryptically.

"You mean for being in love?" she asked with a laugh.

Nash was shocked. "Uh . . . no."

"It's written all over your face," she said. "You don't need to be a psychic to read that." She looked at me and continued to laugh.

I began to blush. But I wasn't about to tell her anything about why we were really there. She was already too interested in werewolves. She'd tried stalking me and Brandon before. I didn't want her to add Nash to her list before we could cure them both.

"No," he said. "That's not why I'm here."

"It's not about love?" she asked. "Most people come here looking for those kinds of answers."

"No. I have this certain condition. . . ."

"Are you sure you don't need to see a medical doctor?" she asked as if she didn't want to be responsible for mistreating something. "Lots of teens have issues, and those are best solved . . ."

"No—" he said. "It's not that, either. Oh . . . I thought you could help me." He began to become frustrated and turned to me. "We better go—this was a mistake."

"I can help," she said. "Please stay. And give me your hand."

Nash turned back and reluctantly extended his hand.

She rubbed her hands together to get them warmed up, her long purple fingernails catching the candlelight. She took his hand and held it. She matched his gaze, then closed her eyes.

"You want to know what to do," she said as if in a trance, "when the full moon comes."

"Yes," he said enthusiastically. "Yes."

She closed her eyes. "I feel here that your love line is very strong," she said, pressing on his palm. "Very strong feelings you have for one particular person."

Nash didn't want to know about his love life. And I didn't want her encouraging him to reunite with me.

"But there is something getting in the way," she continued, "or someone. I sense a strong animal impulse."

She opened her eyes. "It's you," she said as if she was staring at a werewolf.

"It's me what?" Nash was confused. And so was I.

"The wolf. I could feel it. You are the wolf." Dr. Meadows was serious.

"No—" he refused.

"I thought it was the other boy—" she said, looking at me. "But it is you after all."

"I'm not anything!" Nash exclaimed, scooting back.

"I can help you," she said sincerely.

"You can?"

"Yes, at the next full moon. Meet me at Willow Park. I will be there to help you through it."

"No," I said protectively. Not again. Dr. Meadows just wanted to catch a transformation on video so she could become a paranormal star.

Nash wasn't about to wait for her to show up on the next full moon, either. Instead he reached for her again. "Tell me what I'm supposed to do. That's why I am here!"

It was as if Dr. Meadows didn't want to answer him. She wanted to use him for her own gain, just like she wanted to with Brandon.

But Nash was persistent. "Read my hand and tell me the answer I am looking for," he insisted.

"I can help you more if I am there with you."

"You can help me just fine now," he said. "Take my hand." He held his hand out until she had no other choice but to grasp it or walk away.

The psychic realized the severity of the situation. She placed his hand on hers again.

Nash sighed with relief.

Dr. Meadows drew a deep breath, trying to regain her trance mode. It took her a few seconds, but she seemed to be channeling something strong. "I know what it is," she said. "A cure."

"Yes," he said. "Yes!"

"You only have to take it."

"But I don't have one!" he said.

"You must consume it!"

Then she snapped out of it and dropped his hand.

"But I don't have one," he reiterated. "Where do I get it?

Tell me where!" He pushed his hand at her again.

"Your reading is done," she said.

"No, it isn't. You told me to take it. But how do I find it?"

"I only can tell you to consume it."

This time Nash reached across the table and grabbed her hand. "Tell me!"

She was startled by his outburst. She struggled to pull her hand away, but he held on to her until she eventually relented. Then she closed her eyes again.

She paused for a moment, and Nash and I waited with bated breath.

Finally it was as if she was feeling a connection. "It is closer than you think," she said. "Just relax and the answer will unfold. But when the opportunity is revealed to you, the answer is yes. Take it. You will be normal again."

Nash let out a huge sigh of relief. He let go of her hand, stood up, and reached over to the psychic.

"Thank you," he said. He gave her an enthusiastic hug.

Dr. Meadows was startled by his display of affection. She suddenly was swept over by his embrace and became giggly, like any schoolgirl might. "You should come in for readings more often," she said, taken in by Nash's charm.

"This was the only one I needed," he said enthusiastically. We left the room, and he handed her his money.

"And something for the lovely lady, too," Nash declared. "Go on, Celeste. Pick out a necklace." He was so relieved by her prediction, all the sorrow he had been feeling was replaced with joy.

"Thanks anyway," I said. I was happy Nash was pleased and wanted to head to Brandon's before Dr. Meadows gave me any predictions.

"I'll get her something later," he said to Dr. Meadows.

Dr. Meadows was beaming with her happy customer. As we began to leave, Dr. Meadows politely followed us out.

Suddenly I saw purple fingernails on my arm and felt her hand grip me tightly. I tried to shift away before she could say anything to me but her hold was too tight.

She locked her gaze with my own. "Beware of the full moon," she said intensely. "A werewolf wants to take you into his world. Forever."

Nash and I gazed at each other in fear.

Then she released her hand and smiled as if she had only said good-bye.

Nash and I just waved and quickly left the store. Her words echoed in my head over the sounds of the clanging chimes as the door to Penny for Your Thoughts closed behind us.

When we reached our cars, Nash stopped me before I opened my door.

"I want to thank you," he said. "You've done more for me than anyone in my life. Really."

"It's okay." I was eager to leave Dr. Meadows's storefront.

"It was a bit freaky—especially at the end. What do you think she meant?"

"I don't know. I'm sure it meant nothing."

"But what you did meant everything," he said. "She told me I'll get a cure, and I'll be back to normal. I can't wait until that happens. And I have you to thank."

He was still holding my arm, and his fingers began to touch my elbow.

It tickled, and chills ran through me. In a moment, Nash was going to kiss me.

It was enough that I'd gone somewhere alone with him when I was dating Brandon. I couldn't let my former boyfriend kiss me, too.

His warm smile radiated, and it was hard not to be under his spell. But as he leaned in, I pulled back.

"I've done enough today," I said, and opened my door.

Nash waited as I got in and started the engine. As I took off for Brandon's, Nash waved, then headed for the Eastside.

Dr. Meadows's words haunted me. They echoed in my mind. *"Beware of the full moon,"* she had said. *"A werewolf wants to take you into his world. Forever."*

Would Nash try to take me into the werewolf world before he was cured? Was he going to bite me under a full moon and make me transform? Every time I came to Penny for Your Thoughts, I left more frustrated and worried than when I had arrived.

SEVEN

rude boys

As I drove away from Penny for Your Thoughts, I noticed my gas gauge was close to empty, so I pulled into a gas station before I reached Brandon's house, even though I wanted to race to Brandon's side to tell him what Dr. Meadows had told Nash and not miss even a minute more that I could spend with him—especially since Nash had cut into my time with him. I knew that it would be after dark when I left Brandon's, but it was still best to fuel up now.

Abby and Ivy would freak if they knew I was getting gas on the Westside. They thought people on the "wrong" side of town were shady, to say the least. Everyone was really friendly, and all the people I saw looked normal to me. After I fueled up, I went inside the station to pay. An older man was already being helped, so I stood in line behind him. As soon as it was my turn, I looked up and saw a guy standing in my place, as if I hadn't been waiting at all.

The guy appeared to be a junior or senior and sported black, spiky hair, silver piercings, and several tattoos. He wore a brown waffle shirt and oversized blue jeans. He was attractive but obviously not courteous.

I was impatient to get to Brandon's, and I didn't appreciate that this guy had gotten in my way. So I spoke up.

"Excuse me, it's my turn," I said politely.

The spiky-haired guy didn't budge. He didn't even acknowledge me but instead told the clerk what he wanted. I was already riled up after Dr. Meadows's new prediction. I didn't want to become a werewolf—especially one with Nash—and all that it could mean. And this guy was getting on my already frazzled nerves.

"I've been waiting here," I said in the sweetest voice I could muster.

Then he turned around. His hazel eyes gazed up my body as he checked me out ever so slowly, from my sandals to the pink headband in my hair. It creeped me out.

"So?" he responded when he was finished.

"So?" I retorted. "What about being a gentleman?"

"I don't have time for that," he said as he handed the clerk his money.

He turned back to me, this time standing a little too close for my comfort. I couldn't physically move him, and I didn't want to get into an altercation. But I was so surprised—and ticked off—at his rude behavior.

"So are you this rude to everyone?" I asked in a huff.

"I can be worse." He stared into me as if he was daring me to test just how far he could take this.

"Hard to imagine," I shot back.

That made him smile. "So what's your name?"

"I don't have one."

"My name is Ryder."

He grabbed his change and his pack of cigarettes. He didn't appear old enough to buy them, so I assumed he had a fake ID.

"Now it's your turn," he said snidely, gesturing to me to step up to the register. He pretended to tip an imaginary hat.

I gave him one last scowl and broke eye contact with him. He headed out the door.

There were two guys around the same age waiting for him outside. One had fiery ginger hair; the other's was shaggy, long, and blond. For some reason they kept looking back at me. Ryder took out two cigarettes and handed them to his friends. They smoked while he just stared at me. I thought they'd laugh at me, the girl who tried to stand up to the bully, but they didn't. Instead they just smoked and talked, as if they were discussing something important—me. I paused inside the store, pretending to read a mag, to make sure they weren't waiting for me to leave. It seemed like an eternity until they threw their butts on the ground and smashed them with their black boots. They got into their car—a vintage black Firebird—and pulled out. I went quickly to my car and started the engine, then saw them idling at the corner. I sped out of the gas station. Once on the road to Brandon's house, I checked my rearview mirror and was relieved to find they weren't following me.

I'd never seen these guys before in town. And I was hoping that they were just passing through.

When I reached Brandon's guesthouse, he was already waiting outside for me, fixing a broken kitchen chair. "What took you so long?" Brandon asked, looking worried.

"I had to stop for gas. There was this guy at the store who was so rude. He jumped in front of me, and when I said it was my turn, he was like, 'Too bad.'"

"That *is* rude." He wiped his hands and gave me a long, heavenly kiss.

For a moment, I was distracted. But when we stopped, my thoughts turned back to my unusual encounter. I shook my head. "I've never seen anyone like him. He was just so brazenly impolite. He should have had manners."

"Maybe he wasn't taught any. You'll have to let it go. . . ."

"You're right. Maybe I should feel sorry for him instead of angry."

"Yes," he said, gently rubbing my back. "Now tell me what happened at Dr. Meadows's."

I felt even more stressed, like I was going to explode. "Nash had his reading. He wanted to know what to do. He insisted she tell him. He even grabbed her hand. Then she said a cure would be revealed to him and that he should take it. That he would be cured."

"With my dad's serum?" he asked.

"She didn't say. Only that it would be revealed to him. But yes, I think that's what she meant. I don't know of any other cures."

"But my dad wants *me* to take it."

"I know. So you will, and then we can get some for Nash. He'll take it and be cured. Then all our werewolf problems will be solved."

For a moment I fantasized about a life at Legend's Run High as ordinary as any other student's. I'd take my classes and see my boyfriend every day. I'd hang with my friends, and Nash could continue to be the star athlete. Our only problems would be what movie to see on the weekend or what dress I'd wear to the next dance. I had to admit, I'd miss those nights under the full moon when Brandon was so wild and irresistible. But I'd forgo those extraordinary times for the chance for him to live a normal life again.

"That's great news," he said excitedly. Then he changed his tone. "If you believe in that stuff."

"Well, usually I don't. But she's been right before. . . . But then, it is Dr. Meadows. She wants someone to become a werewolf—so she can get her camera out, tape it, show it to the world, and become famous. And she has more to gain with Nash being a werewolf full-time. Do you think she told him to take it to become a werewolf full-time?"

"Isn't that unethical?"

"Yes. It is. But she was trying to use us when I told her about you."

"She did do that."

"But she was touching him when she gave him that advice. I think she must have really been channeling something."

"Well, if she gives wrong advice, then she has more to worry about than anyone, don't you think? She'd be putting herself in harm's way if she told him to take it, knowing he'd transform every night."

"I guess you're right," I said, sort of relieved.

"And if she predicts he will be cured—then I assume that means . . ."

"That you will be, too."

He smiled. "Then I can be. If we believe her."

"Yes."

"But she didn't say I would be, too."

"No, but I assume so. You are going to take it first, right? Nash can't be cured until you are."

Brandon put his arm around me. I sensed the relief he was feeling, and I could only figure he was imagining our lives together without being a werewolf, just as I had a moment ago. However, there were other predictions Dr. Meadows warned of, and I wasn't too keen on being the one to shake him out of his good mood.

He gave me a luscious kiss.

I couldn't make eye contact with him.

"What's wrong?" he asked. "Isn't this good news—if it's true?"

"Yes," I said. "But there's also the other thing she said." I chewed my lip as I decided how to tell him about the last prediction she had made. "Nash is going to bite me," I finally blurted out.

"He's going to do what?" he asked, half laughing. "I thought you went there to find out if he's going to be cured."

"It's not a joke. I think Nash is going to bite me and turn me into a werewolf."

"Why would you think that? Did Dr. Meadows say that?"

"Sort of."

"Slow down." He put his arm around me and guided me to a picnic bench in his grandparents' backyard. We sat on the tabletop. "Now, tell me everything."

"When I left, she said, 'Beware of the full moon. A werewolf wants to take you into his world. Forever.'"

"That can mean a lot of things," Brandon surmised.

"It means one thing. Nash is going to turn me into a werewolf. I'm the next one in line."

Brandon thought for a moment. "What—how is he going to take you into his world?" he asked.

"He could bite me. You've seen him when he changes. He's violent."

"But now he's aware of himself when he's a werewolf. We were hoping your kiss would cure him of the thoughtless violence."

"I know. But that was before Dr. Meadows made this horrible prediction."

"What if she's not talking about *that* werewolf? What if she means me?"

"What do you mean?" I asked. I hadn't even thought of Brandon.

"Maybe she is warning you that I'm going to hurt you—bite you. Maybe the warning was about me." Brandon was visibly disturbed. He stood and paced around the table.

"Why would you hurt me?" I asked. "You haven't before. I've been with you a bunch of times when you were in lycan form. But Nash—he's tried to attack me at least two times. The next full moon is coming soon, Brandon. What if he finds me?"

"It's okay," he reassured me. He came back and sat beside me.

I was really scared. My life seemed to be spinning in chaos. The thought of my becoming a werewolf? My hands began to tremble.

I was so shaken up by the visit, the prediction, and the rude boy, I began to cry. I wanted our love life to be easier. Do homework together, kiss and cuddle, take walks in the woods. Now it was spiraling out of control. I felt like I was in danger.

Brandon held me tightly as I wiped away tears that streamed down my face.

"I was scared when you first turned," I said. "Then again when Nash did. Now I'm scared again."

"Maybe you shouldn't have gone to Dr. Meadows. She puts horrible thoughts in your head. And who says she's right?"

"She's been right all along," I argued. "I knew I shouldn't have gone with Nash. But I felt sad for him. And now look what has happened."

"But what does she know, really?" Brandon proposed.

"Uh . . . everything! She's been right about *everything*. And if I'd listened to her from the beginning, I wouldn't have walked home alone. . . ."

"And, I know . . . I wouldn't have been bitten," Brandon said as if finishing my sentence.

"It's true," I said. "She said it first and then it happened."

Brandon paused. I knew he didn't believe in Dr. Meadows's predictions, but my nervousness was making him rethink the issue.

"Then we have to do something about it."

"Do what?" I asked.

"We have to let Nash take the serum," Brandon said firmly to me, "on the night of the next full moon. He'll come here, and I'll give it to him. We have to—if not for his sake, then for yours."

"Really?" I asked. "You decided . . . you were going to take it. Finally."

"But we didn't know about this. And now I can't take that chance."

I realized what he was really giving up: the cure for himself. "But that means you'll still be a werewolf."

"Well, if it means you won't, then I'm game."

"But your father—you promised you'd be the one who takes it first."

"That was before I knew about this prediction. If you say she's been right before, then we can't chance it this time. He can't change you into a werewolf if he isn't one."

"And your father was counting on me to make sure you took it. I don't know what to do. I don't want to let him down," I said.

"You don't have to worry about that. You have enough on your plate besides worrying about my father's feelings."

"So Nash will take the dose you have and then you'll get your father to make you another dose for the following full moon?"

"Yes," he said reassuringly.

"I just wanted us to be together," I said. "I wanted you to be normal—for your own sake. And now you won't be. . . . It seems to get more chaotic every day."

Brandon appeared content. I think he was relieved to be helping out Nash and me at the same time when, in fact, I wanted to be the one who was helping Brandon.

The following day after school, I saw Nash and tried to catch him before he went to practice.

"I'm not sure you should be near me anymore," he said. "What Dr. Meadows said at the end . . . You can't be around me anymore."

"Well, I have to be," I insisted. "I have something to tell you."

"Don't get too close," he said. "The moon will be full soon. I don't know what I'll do now."

"You won't do anything now but listen," I commanded.

"Sit down." I pulled him aside on the steps to the side entrance of school. "We might have a cure."

"What?"

"Brandon's father is a scientist. He made a possible antidote."

"Are you kidding? This is great!"

"Brandon's father made it for *him*."

"Oh . . . yes, that makes sense."

"His father was just in town. And Brandon told him about you. He asked for a second batch for you."

"Brandon did that for me?" Nash was taken aback.

I nodded. "Yes. There is only one vial now."

"Oh," he said. "But that still is great news."

"You think so?" I asked. I wasn't sure how Nash would respond—if he'd be hopeful or competitive that Brandon might be cured first.

"One less werewolf," he said with a smile. "And then if it works for him . . ."

"It can work for you," I assured him.

"I appreciate you telling me this." He leaned in and gave me a friendly hug. He was so relieved I could feel his tension releasing in our embrace.

"I have something else to tell you," I said when he pulled away.

"What?"

"Brandon wants you to take it first."

"What? Why? Because of Dr. Meadows's prediction?"

I reluctantly nodded.

"Why does he think I'll be the one to bite you?"

"We both think so. I've been around Brandon for several full moons. He hasn't hurt me at all. He's only been kinder, even."

"And I've been a monster."

"No . . ."

"I remember, Celeste. I remember everything."

We were both quiet for a minute, neither one of us wanting to talk about the horrible ways he'd acted before.

Nash finally smiled and broke the silence. "Of course I'll take it. I can't believe he's going to give it to me." He paused, really taking in Brandon's generosity. "I owe him big-time! Maybe I can get him a spot on the team."

I felt relieved that Nash was going to take the serum and that he was grateful to Brandon. Nash was not only changing as a werewolf but as a human being, too—he was becoming much more gracious.

Later that day, Brandon and I were settling into his guesthouse room. He was placing his backpack on his computer table and I was laying my sweater over his chair when we heard Apollo barking and a car pull up the long drive.

"Your grandparents must be home," I said.

Brandon rose and peeked out the window. "That's not my grandparents," he said.

He pulled back the curtain even farther. It was a BMW.

What was Nash doing at Brandon's? He never came to this side of town if he didn't have to. But I had an inkling as to why he was making such a sudden appearance.

Brandon opened the door and stepped out as I hopped off the chair. It was as if he thought I might be threatened and was heading Nash off at the pass. I tried to follow behind him.

Nash got out of his car and walked toward my boyfriend.

Apollo continued to bark. Nash had always been afraid of dogs—and at the very least shied away from them. So when Apollo raced for Nash, I was sure he'd step back a few feet. However, Nash didn't budge.

Brandon called out to Apollo, but he didn't retreat. Instead Nash just watched Apollo as the husky proceeded straight for him. When the dog reached Nash, Nash looked down at him with an intense stare. Apollo winced and raced back to Brandon, cowering behind him.

Nash continued to walk toward Brandon. "Hey, dude," Nash said in a friendly voice.

"Hey—" Brandon answered.

"Celeste told me . . . about the cure," Nash said.

"Keep your voice down!" Brandon chided. No one was around, but I could feel my boyfriend's tension about even the birds knowing his lycan identity.

"And Celeste says you are giving it to me," he said, lowering his voice.

"Yes. I am."

Nash was obviously touched. "I can't believe that you'd do that for me."

"I have *something*, but it's only a possible cure," Brandon said.

"A possible one is better than none at all."

"I don't know if it works," Brandon confessed.

"I still can't believe you are going to give it to me," Nash said. "What's the worst that can happen?"

"Well, there's no guarantee it will work, honestly. You might end up a werewolf full-time."

"Celeste didn't tell me that part."

I felt awkward. "I wanted to—"

"It's okay," he said. "It's a chance we have to take," Nash insisted. "If it works for me, then it will work for you."

Nash was showing a milder, more generous side. It was as if becoming a werewolf had made him more understanding as a human.

"Come here next Friday, just before the first night of the full moon," Brandon said. "I will have it for you to take."

Nash shook Brandon's hand, got back into his car, and drove off. I leaned into Brandon and gave him a huge hug.

Brandon and I took a walk in his backyard. But even when we stopped to admire the several deer we spotted in the woods or when we shared a few passionate kisses, the cure and its possible side effects were never too far from our thoughts.

We were nestled together by a tree as the sun was setting. Brilliant shades of reds and orange hovered over the treetops in a spectacular display. It was breathtaking as we kissed and cuddled.

When we drew apart, Brandon brushed the hair away from my face. He gazed lovingly at my eyes, my cheeks, my lips.

"It's still hard for me to get your kiss with Nash out of my head," Brandon said suddenly. "At times, I'm glad he's a werewolf! Serves him right."

"It's okay. It's only natural to have those feelings. If I saw you kiss Hayley," I said, referring to the skater chick on the Westside who was fond of Brandon, "I'd lose it!"

"Well . . ."

"You really did such a nice thing for Nash," I said.

"Maybe this whole thing will be over very soon. If Nash is cured, I can be next in line."

"And then the Legend's Run werewolves will be extinct," I said.

I leaned against him and rubbed his shoulder.

He took me into his embrace and nuzzled against me. "You'll still bring out the animal in me," he laughed. "I don't think that will change."

I giggled as he tickled me.

"What do you think our world will be like when I'm cured?" he asked.

"I guess it would be like this," I said. "Us hanging out and doing everyday stuff."

"You'd be satisfied with that?" he asked seriously. "Me just being a regular guy?"

"You'll never be regular," I assured him.

"Actually I bet you can't wait. Dating a werewolf—a freak—I'm so lucky you've stood by me."

"Of course," I said. "But it hasn't been all bad. There are some things I like about being with a werewolf."

"Really?" he asked, like my feelings were unimaginable. "Like what?"

"Like when you save little boys from a pack of wolves."

"You liked that?"

I nodded enthusiastically. "And you're really strong. Your muscles are killer, and you run so fast."

"So, if I take the serum, you think I'll just be a weak troll?" he teased.

"I didn't mean that," I said.

He thought for a moment, I assumed reflecting on his time as a lycan. "I won't be able to see in the night. Or sleep outside among the stars without protection."

"And no more wolves following us around like pets," I added.

He gazed up at the waxing moon.

"Yes, I love that wolf pack. They are really so gentle and protective," he lamented.

"You like being a werewolf, don't you?" I hinted.

"Of course not." Brandon sat up as if I'd spoken out of turn.

"No, it's okay," I tried to assure him. "You can tell me. You like the outdoors. And this does provide you with an insight into the animal world that most people don't get to experience."

He paused and then relaxed a bit. "Yes, I guess," he said, thinking.

Maybe I was the one wanting to continue his life as a werewolf. Did I like him so much in that form that I was missing how it was making him feel?

"You make me sound like I enjoy being a monster," Brandon said.

"You aren't a monster," I assured him, and gave him a hug. "You're something extraordinary. With and without a full moon."

"Well, hopefully we'll eventually put an end to my life as a werewolf."

EIGHT

girls and gangs

We saw you following Nash away from school the other day," Ivy said the next day at the mall when we met by the food court for some girl time after school.

"You did?" I asked. I was surprised they noticed and wasn't prepared to talk about it.

"Yes. Where were you guys going?" Abby asked.

"Yeah, what's going on? A secret rendezvous with your old boyfriend?" Ivy teased.

"Does Brandon know about this?" Abby said as if she was worried about my boyfriend's feelings.

"Yes, he knows," I said.

They both paused. "So you did go somewhere with Nash?" Ivy said. "Do tell."

"It was no biggie. Really." But the fact was it really was major news. Nash was a werewolf, and he wanted to see if he'd ever be cured. But now that he knew there was a possible antidote and he'd be taking it on the upcoming full moon, he was a much happier person.

However, I couldn't tell them about Dr. Meadows. They would want to know all sorts of information, and I was hoping to skate through the next week without incident. We only had a little over a week until the full moon appeared and I didn't need any more drama with my friends.

"Where did you guys go?" Ivy insisted.

"Did you make out?" Abby raised her eyebrows.

"No," I said. I wasn't one to lie—I always cracked a smile when I tried to even tell the slightest fib; or worse, I would break out in a rash. But I couldn't tell them what we really did.

"He just wanted to talk. That's all," I said.

"About what?" Abby asked.

I sighed. I hung out with Abby and Ivy to get my mind off my troubles. Instead they were pushing me back to the difficult thoughts of werewolves. I knew my friends would be persistent. I wasn't sure why I expected anything else.

"Ooh, there are those guys again," Ivy said.

"What guys?" I was happy to have the subject switched from me and Nash to anything else.

"Those thugs," Ivy said, pointing down to the first level. "Totally gross!"

I saw the backs of a few guys talking to a pretty girl with a few shopping bags, but I couldn't tell who they were.

"We saw them yesterday outside the coffee shop. It was like they were deliberately pushing our buttons," Ivy said.

"Maybe they were flirting," I said.

"Didn't seem so. They were asking us strange questions," Abby said.

"What sort of questions?" I asked.

"All sorts. Did we like the outdoors?" Ivy remembered.

"They asked me if I liked wolves," Abby added.

"That *is* weird," I said.

"We didn't answer, just ignored them and walked on. Eventually they left us alone." Ivy took a breath. "This one guy had tatts and spiky hair," she said. "He was totally gross."

"I thought he was cute," Abby said, defending him.

"You did?" Ivy asked, making a disgusted face. "You would."

When the girl moved on, the guys turned around. They were in plain view. I stepped closer to see them below. It was Ryder and his two friends. I froze. They seemed to be scanning the shoppers for something—or someone. Ryder continued to eye the shoppers, then suddenly glanced up and caught sight of me watching him. I lost my breath. He stared at me as if he'd found what he was looking for. Just then Ivy pulled me toward the store and out of view.

"Uh . . . we have to leave," I said anxiously.

"Why? We haven't even bought anything yet," Ivy whined.

"I don't know. We just do." I felt weird with those guys in the mall. Even with hundreds of people in the same place, I didn't feel safe. I must have appeared as if I'd spotted a hungry zombie.

"What's wrong?" Ivy asked me.

"I've seen them before, too," I confessed.

"You did?" Ivy was shocked. She put her hands on her hips. "Where?"

"At the convenience store when I was getting gas."

"Which one?" Ivy asked.

"The one in Westside."

"I meant which guy." Ivy rolled her eyes.

"Oh . . . Ryder."

"You know his name?" Abby asked, intrigued.

"Why were you getting gas in the Westside?" Ivy asked.

"I was on my way to Brandon's."

"You shouldn't be stopping there," she warned.

"Who cares why she was there? How do you know his name?" Abby wondered.

"He was bugging me—he was really rude. But then he introduced himself."

"That's weird," Ivy said. "Promise you won't go there anymore."

"He was trying to pick you up," Abby said. "He *likes* you."

"I wouldn't want to go out with him," I scoffed. "Can we just leave?"

"Why? They won't bother us again," Abby said. "I'm not going to let them spoil a good day of shopping."

"What if they come back to bother us?" I asked.

"Then I'll kick them with my brand-new heels," Abby said, holding a Macy's bag.

"Seriously," I said.

Abby glanced around. "They're gone."

I inched a few steps toward the glass overlook; they'd disappeared.

"I wonder who they are," Abby said.

"We know one of them is Ryder," Ivy retorted.

"They aren't from around here, I know that," Abby said. "They don't go to school here, and they appear to be around our age."

"Maybe they are juvies or homeless."

"They seem like they are searching for something," Abby said.

"Trouble," Ivy said emphatically.

Suddenly we spotted them coming up the escalator only fifty feet away.

Ivy gasped. Then she pulled us into a lingerie store.

"Why do we have to hide in here?" Abby said.

"They just spotted me," I said. "I feel really weird."

We hurried to the back of the store and hung out behind a display of bras.

The guys came in.

"Can I help you?" a saleswoman asked them.

Ryder paused. "You? No, I'm not looking for you."

"They *are* following us!" Ivy said.

The woman gave him a puzzled expression as he glanced around.

"Did you see a girl with a pink headband in here?"

"Honey, they all have headbands," she said. "Feel free to check around."

The saleswoman walked away from the guys and helped another customer.

Abby tugged at our shirts. "Quick," she said, and we raced into a fitting room.

She locked the door, and we all stood on the bench.

Ivy was panicking. Sure, we didn't know these guys, and no, he hadn't done anything to us besides being rude, but their vibe was deadly.

"Shh!" Abby said. She put her hands over Ivy's mouth.

We could see a shadow move by the door. Then it paused. Black boots poked through the bottom of our door.

We all held our breath. I thought Ivy or I would faint.

"What is he doing here?" Abby whispered. "This is the ladies' changing room!"

Abby was ready to open the door and attack but I held her back.

We were filled with fear as we waited.

Then Ivy's cell phone rang.

Ivy tried to cover her phone when the boots disappeared.

"Jake?" Ivy whispered. "These weird guys are following us. Can you come to the mall, now?"

Abby opened the door and peeked her head out. "All clear."

We sneaked out of the room and peered into the store. When we didn't see them, we walked through the aisles until we reached the entrance. We all gazed around; fortunately the guys were nowhere in sight.

"That was so creepy!" Ivy said.

"What does he want?" I asked.

"I think he wants you," Abby said, turning to me.

"Why?" I asked. "Why would you say that?"

"Because he asked the clerk for you. You're wearing a pink headband."

"I don't know why he wants me," I said, freaked out.

"It's okay," Ivy said, putting her arm around my shoulder. "He's gone. Let's banish those losers from our minds. Jake will be here soon. We have real men to talk about. What's up with you and Brandon?"

He's going to turn into a werewolf in a few days, I wanted to say. As if I didn't have enough to deal with already. ·

I texted Brandon about meeting us at the mall, but he responded that he was taking his grandmother to the doctor.

We waited until Jake and Dylan met us outside the store. They hung out with us as we continued to shop. Ivy's and Abby's minds quickly were distracted with things they could add to their spring wardrobes.

I, however, had two particular things on my mind. Who was this Ryder guy, and what did he want with me?

I met Brandon at his house after the mall. I was preoccupied by my frightening experience but was so relieved when I saw my handsome and strong boyfriend standing outside his guesthouse. I rushed to him and gave him a hug, my body caving into his. Apparently I couldn't hide my worries from Brandon, as he immediately gave me a curious look.

"Sorry I couldn't meet you at the mall. Your text sounded strange. Weren't you girls having fun?"

"That rude guy from the gas station was there."

"Really?"

"He was following us."

"He was?"

"Yes, he gives me the creeps," I said with a shudder.

"Are you sure he is really following you? Or could it just be a coincidence?" he asked in a tone that was trying to soothe me.

"He was bothering Ivy and Abby, too," I continued. "They must be a gang of some sort. He was trying to talk to other girls at the mall as well. It's like he's trying to test us— or find someone special."

"Well, you are special," he said.

"I'm serious. He saw Ivy, Abby, and me at the mall. When we ducked into a store, he followed us in there. He even followed us into the girls' changing area."

Brandon was visibly disturbed by this. He immediately changed his tone. "That is weird. I wonder why he's doing that. I don't want you out of my sight," he said protectively.

"Then you'll have to stay at my house and accompany me everywhere?" I asked coyly.

"I can do that," he said.

"You can have a bed right next to mine."

"I'll watch you all night."

"Would you?"

"I would be glad to," he said. I leaned against his chest, comfortably engulfed by his protective arms. "If he comes near you again, I'm going to release the wolves."

I felt relieved that Brandon was here with me. Without him I would be even more nervous. However, thinking about Ryder following us into the changing room area really made me anxious.

I looked up at my handsome boyfriend. "He wants something, Brandon," I said. "And I think it's me."

"Well, he can't have you," he said, stroking my cheek. "Someone already does."

He leaned into me and kissed my fearful thoughts away.

When I got home, I still couldn't completely shake off the odd behavior of Ryder and his crew. I knew he wasn't from around here—and it was unusual for three students to transfer to a new school together. And since they hadn't shown up at school, it made them all the more intriguing.

I decided to take Champ for a walk and calm my nerves. As we headed down my street, Champ began to bark. I saw someone standing by the wooded area about fifty yards away. It was hard to make out who it was from my vantage point. I was hoping it was Brandon.

Champ continued to bark. "It's okay, boy," I said.

I knew Nash was acting squirrely, so I assumed it was him.

But as I drew closer, I didn't see Nash's blond hair or

even someone unfamiliar. It wasn't Nash. And it wasn't even Dr. Meadows. Or a stranger. It was just someone strange. I gasped and held on tightly to Champ's leash. I couldn't believe my eyes. Fear ran through my flesh, and my heart began to pound out of my chest.

"Ryder?" I said, startled.

"You remembered my name," he said with a churlish smile.

"Why are you following me?"

"I wasn't."

"Then what are you doing here?"

"Walking. Same as you."

"I was going—" But then I realized I didn't want to tell him where I was going. I didn't want him to know where I lived, in case he was stalking me. "Where are *you* going?" I asked.

"You are the curious one. Most girls would have ignored me by this point. But you . . . you're inquisitive. I like that." He eyed me closely, his gaze sending chills down my spine.

"I'd like to know why you are here. That's all."

"What if I said I was trying to talk to you?" He was coy and quizzical.

I was stunned that now he was so candid. That he admitted to it, and that my gut was right. "Why?" I asked as I inched away.

"Uh . . . I thought you were cute the other day." He grinned a sheepish grin. Ryder didn't budge; his confidence was as intriguing to me as much as it made me anxious.

"Thank you, but I'm not interested." I tried to say it politely—enough to let him know where I stood but not too coarse to upset him.

I snuck my cell phone out of my purse and pressed the button to speed dial Brandon.

I waited for a moment, then said loudly, "Well, I gotta go. It's probably best that you go on your way, too. Legend's Run can be sort of dangerous at this time of day."

"Are you serious?" he said. "This is the sunny suburbs. Nothing happens here."

"Well, let's keep it that way." I said again in a loud voice.

Ryder stepped closer. He locked his gaze with mine; I felt as if he would kiss me if he could. "I'm looking for someone. Someone like you."

Just then I heard a car approaching. I was hoping it was someone I knew—one of our neighbors. If so, they might stop and notice I was talking to a stranger. I felt as awkward in the open with Ryder as I did alone in the woods that snowy day with the wolves. But they passed by.

I clenched my fist.

Suddenly I heard another car coming down the street. I was so relieved as this one was familiar.

Ivy was driving her SUV and stopped alongside of me, where I was standing on the sidewalk. "What's going on?" she asked as she and Abby hopped out.

I thought I'd dialed Brandon—but instead I had dialed my best friend. Thank goodness she got the message and lived so close.

"What are you doing here?" Ivy asked Ryder.

"I came to town to see the Legend's Run Werewolf Festival. Is that a crime?"

"No, I mean, what are you doing *here*?" she reiterated.

Two figures emerged from the same woods Ryder had come out of.

"Again, I'm here for the fest," he said with a grin.

"Well, it doesn't start for a few more days, and it still doesn't explain why you are bothering our friend." Ivy was forceful and protective.

"Yes," Abby said in her toughest voice.

"I'm sorry if that's the way it appeared," Ryder said, softening. "I was just hoping to make some new friends while I was in town."

"Well, we have enough friends," Ivy said.

Now Ryder's two friends were close behind him.

Champ continued to bark even louder.

"Well, perhaps you can squeeze in a few more," Ryder said.

Champ began to growl.

Ryder stared at Champ, his gaze fixed with intensity. Champ stopped growling and sat down quietly.

I was shocked. Brandon was able to do this all the time, and Nash had done the same thing only a few days ago to a barking Apollo. It wasn't normal. There could be only one reason Ryder had the power to do that.

I held on to Champ's leash and moved back a few inches.

Ivy and Abby seemed puzzled.

"What are you, a dog whisperer?" Abby asked.

"Of sorts," he said cryptically.

I didn't let on that I knew who—or what—he was. I couldn't say it in front of my friends.

"What were you doing in the woods?" Ivy said.

"Hunting," the blond said with a laugh.

"You can't hunt here!" Abby scolded.

"We don't use guns," the redhead chimed in.

I felt creeped out by their insinuations, and I knew what they were talking about.

"I don't care what you use," Abby said. "You need to go back where you came from."

"We're planning on being here for a bite longer . . . I mean bit," the blond said. The gang laughed at his joke.

"You guys are juvies," Ivy said. "We have better things to do than talk to you. C'mon, girls, let's go."

"Wait—" Ryder said. "We got off on the wrong foot." He held out his hand.

"I'm Ryder and this is Leopold," he said, referring to the scraggly blond. "And this is Hunter," he said, gesturing toward the fiery redhead.

The two guys waved and smiled.

"Hunter?" Abby said with a laugh. "Seems appropriate."

"Nice to meet you," Ivy said, polite enough. "But we have to be going." She pulled me and Abby away from the guys and toward the SUV.

But Ryder jogged after us.

"We wanted to know if you ladies would like to go out

sometime," Ryder said, catching up to us at the car.

Abby turned and gazed up at him. It wasn't the first time guys had ever flirted with us, and she always seemed to get a rise out of it. "Our calendar is filled," she said to him coyly.

"Well, maybe you can cancel a few things," he insisted.

"Uh . . . I think not," Ivy said. "We really have to go."

Then Ryder stepped toward me. "What about you?" he asked, staring straight at me.

"She has a boyfriend," Abby said for me. "And he's really big and strong."

"Can't she speak for herself?" Ryder asked.

"Listen," Ivy began. "You leave her alone. Leave us alone."

"I don't know what tricks you put on to her dog. You must have one of those whistles that only dogs hear," Abby said.

Ryder just smiled.

"And wolves, too," Leopold said.

I could tell that Abby liked the attention slightly and couldn't help but flirt back with the guys. But I didn't want to give them any passes to hang out with us now or in the future.

"I'm sure you can find three single girls in town who would love to hang out with you guys," Ivy finally said.

"You think so?" Hunter said.

"Absolutely."

"I'm not so sure," Abby challenged with a mischievous smile. Everything was a game to her, and this was no exception.

"Yes, there will be some," Ivy said. "We've got to go."

"Are you so sure?" Hunter asked.

"Come on, Ivy," I said. "It's been lovely talking but we have to get home and study. We have school, you know."

"We hope to see you again," Ryder said.

"In your dreams," Ivy muttered.

Ryder's comment left a feeling of uneasiness inside me. They hung back as we got into the SUV.

When we were safely inside, we turned around. The guys were gone.

I petted Champ, who growled as he stared toward the woods.

"Those guys were creepy!" Ivy said as she drove off.

"I know. I wonder what they want," I said. The idea that Ryder could possibly be a werewolf frightened me. The full moon was only a week away.

"Yes, total stalkers," Ivy said. "Like they have nothing to do but hang out in malls—and now the woods—accosting girls?"

"I think that Ryder guy was hot. They all were," said Abby. She leaned against her seat, dreaming. "If I wasn't going out with Dylan, I might like Ryder. Or maybe Hunter. Or maybe Leopold. Which one would you like?" she said to Ivy.

"Gross, Abby! Besides, I love Jake."

"Duh. I know that, but if not."

"Ooh," she said. "Not going there."

"C'mon, Ivy!" Abby said. "You have to pick one."

"Well, I guess I'd choose the redhead. I thought he was cute. I mean, no, I don't!"

"You do!" Abby squealed.

"Now you, Celeste."

"Yes, we've both done it," Ivy said, looking in the rear-view mirror.

"Who would you choose?" Abby pressed.

I couldn't bear to think about anyone besides Brandon. "Brandon is the only guy for me," I said.

Ivy pulled into Abby's driveway and turned off the engine.

"But if he didn't exist," Abby said.

"I don't know—"

"You have to say. We did," Ivy insisted. "I'm not letting you out until you do." She pressed the locks on the car.

Ryder was different. He was unlike any guy in town—or that I'd ever seen. He was edgy and had piercings and tattoos. I was intrigued by his style and brazen attitude, though put off by his rude behavior. Now that my friends put me on the spot, I couldn't help but wonder what I'd think of him if I hadn't met Brandon. I thought long and hard. The three guys were each hot in their own right. But there was one who looked a lot like the guy I was already in love with. "Ryder," I said.

"I knew it!" Abby said. "There's a connection there."

"There is not."

"I could feel it," she went on. "He is so hot for you!"

"No he's not. Don't say that. I love Brandon."

"Leave her alone," Ivy told Abby.

"He doesn't even know me," I said.

"He doesn't have to. It's your beauty and aura," Abby teased.

Ivy unlocked the doors and we all got out. We went into Abby's house, and Pumpkin and Champ played around as we ate pizza. I continued to be distracted by our new situation. I think we had just come in contact with three more handsome, but freaky, werewolves.

When I got home, I had a hard time shaking Ryder from my thoughts. The way he stared at me was no longer creepy—it was intense. It was as if he knew me—or wanted to know me. The part that bothered me was that it was slightly thrilling. He was so intense and confident, it was attractive.

I'd also never been exposed to someone like him. Was he a hood or a thug or just a misunderstood teen? He was the opposite of anyone I'd ever been attracted to in my life. He lived on the edge, and though this usually turned me off, I found in this case I was battling myself because this time it didn't.

I'd had a crush on Nash for a few years before we dated. He was handsome. Popular. A basketball star.

And I was so in love with Brandon, sometimes I couldn't

see straight. I loved everything about him: the way he was compassionate toward animals, the times he helped his grandmother with groceries, how he wasn't afraid to put his life in harm's way. He really was the most courageous guy I'd ever known.

Ryder was also something out of the ordinary. I wasn't sure why he was so interested in me. I might not give him a second thought, since I was already in love with someone else, but there was this magnetic pull I had toward him that I couldn't shake. His edgy personality and intensity stuck with me; I was having a hard time getting him out of my mind.

I wondered what it would be like if I'd never met Brandon or Nash—that I'd met Ryder instead. Would I be the kind of girl who would be pulled to someone who was so unlike myself? And live on the wild side with a dangerous and daring guy with spiky hair, tattoos, and more earrings than I wore?

But I was in love with someone—and it wasn't him. It was Brandon. A handsome, rugged gentleman in his own right, with integrity and a zest for life and nature that appealed to me way more than a reckless, back-talking, attractive punk. I reminisced about being held in Brandon's powerful embrace and being lost when our lips touched and melted together. It wasn't long before I forgot all about a guy named Ryder.

NINE

wicked werewolves

I wasn't able to see Brandon until the following day at school, and I was so hungry to tell him the latest details.

"Remember those weird guys that I saw at the convenience store and the mall? They showed up near my house." We sat on the school's front steps as I told Brandon all about what had transpired.

"I wish I had known what was going on at the mall," he said. "I would have jumped out of the doctor's office and come right away."

"You had a good reason to be somewhere else. Is your grandmother all right?" I asked.

"I should be asking if *you* are okay."

"Yes, I'm okay." I smiled sweetly. "What did the doctor say about her?"

"To beware of the full moon."

I was stunned. But then he grinned, and we both laughed.

"It was just her annual checkup," Brandon went on. "I can't believe I wasn't there for you," he lamented.

"It's okay. I'm fine. Just a bit shaken up."

"Who are these guys?" he wondered. "Why have they come to town? And why are they bothering you?"

"One of them said that they've come for the Legend's Run Werewolf Fest."

"But that's a week away."

"I know. But I might know why. I think they are werewolves."

"You do?" he asked with concern. "Why?"

"The way one of them eyed Champ. Champ was barking and growling. Then Ryder stared at him, and Champ lay down as if he were ready for a nap. It's the same skill you've had since you transformed. Nash did it to Apollo, too, remember?"

Brandon turned away from me as if he was really hit by this news. "There are more werewolves than just me and Nash?"

I nodded. "I think so."

"This can't have happened," Brandon said. "How?"

"I don't know. But I am convinced that they are werewolves."

"This can't be happening," Brandon reiterated.

"I'm freaking out, too," I conceded. "And what if they aren't like you and Nash? You saw it—Nash isn't the same kind of werewolf you are. He's mean. These guys are rude by day—imagine what they'd be like if they turn at night?"

"We have enough to deal with already." Brandon was clearly worried. "This isn't fair. How can we handle everything at once?"

I was overwhelmed, too. "We'll have to think of something. They said they were looking for new friends. I think I know what they mean."

He turned to me. "You?"

I nodded again. "I'm afraid."

"I won't let anyone hurt you."

"I know that. But what if they want all of us? You can't be everywhere!"

"Nash will be taking the serum soon. Then at least he will hopefully be normal. But now you think there are more? I haven't got a cure for all of us."

"I don't know if that is what they're after. They seem like a gang. I think they might be searching for more members."

"More werewolves?"

"I know. . . . They seemed so interested in me—and Ivy and Abby. I can't have my friends in jeopardy."

"What do we do?" he wondered, frustrated.

"Maybe we should ask Nash to wait to take the cure in case we need help with these new werewolves."

"I can't ask him that."

"I know. I will," I said.

"We can handle this alone. I can handle this alone."

"I'm not sure we have that choice. Dr. Meadows warned

me—so if it isn't you or Nash . . . it might be—"

"One of them?" he asked.

I was truly frightened. My eyes filled with tears. My whole life was so far out of hand.

"We need to find them before the full moon," Brandon said just as first bell rang.

After class, I caught up to Nash at his locker.

"I need to talk to you," I said hurriedly.

"Me first," he said. "I want to tell you and Brandon thank you. I've been acting so strangely lately. I know it's the full moon approaching. But the only thing that is saving me from going crazy is knowing that I'll be able to take that serum."

"That's what I want to talk to you about."

He paused. "He doesn't have it?"

"No, he does."

Nash was relieved. But then his bright expression darkened. "He's not going to let me have it?"

"Can you just listen?"

"Fine. Go ahead," he said impatiently. "But I do want to say this: When I am normal, things can be right again between us. He'll still be a werewolf—with all the unpredictable events that go along with it. But you should be with someone you can count on. You deserve that, Celeste."

"I appreciate your looking out for me," I said as sweetly as I could. "But this isn't about us. You understand I am with Brandon—whether he is a werewolf or not."

He rolled his eyes. "A guy can try."

"I need you to understand that." I wanted Nash to know where we stood—for now and the future—and do it in a kind and sympathetic way.

"Yes. Yes," he said. "I do."

"But I need your help this time. For me."

"Okay. Just tell me."

"There is something that happened in the last few days."

"What happened?"

"These guys that came to town—you might have heard about them from Ivy and Abby. They are here for the Werewolf Festival."

"Are they the creepers?"

"Yes. That's them."

"Did they bother you?"

"Yes. And I'm afraid of them."

He gazed at me earnestly. "Me, Jake, and Dylan can straighten them out," he said. "I have no problem kicking their—"

"You don't have to do that."

"I can," Nash said, his chest puffed out.

"I know. But there is something else you can do."

"What?"

"Don't take the serum on the full moon," I said, looking at him with my eyes wide and pleading.

"Are you insane? Why would I do that?"

"Nash, I think they might not be just regular guys."

"Then what kind of guys are they?"

"I think they are werewolves."

Nash was shocked. As if he couldn't comprehend any more werewolves other than him and Brandon.

I stared at him intently. "And I think they are searching for others—girls—to join their pack."

"How did you get that in your head?"

"This one guy—Ryder—stared down Champ like you did Apollo, like Brandon did in the wolf enclosure at the zoo. The only humans I've seen who can do that are also werewolves."

"How can that be?" he asked. "More werewolves in town? I've never even heard of this Ryder guy."

"They are from Huntington. And I think they want to try to turn me."

This time Nash was the calm one, being helpful to me. "You don't know for sure that they really are werewolves."

"I do, Nash. I've seen it with you and Brandon. I know what these guys are. And remember Dr. Meadows's prediction? If you aren't the one who is going to bite me, that means one of them is."

"So we'll have to do something," he said. "No one is going to hurt you."

I felt relieved by his protectiveness toward me and decided I could ask him the tough question. "Will you delay taking the serum until the following full moon? I need you to be as fast and strong as they are so Brandon will not be all alone. You have to be on Brandon's side, as a werewolf, in case they try anything crazy."

He scooted back and looked away. Then he leaned in again. "I can help—and I will help. But as a human."

"What? You won't wait?"

"I can't wait. I have to be normal again."

"But can't you even at least think about it?" I asked.

He put his hand on mine. "I can do more as myself than I can as a werewolf, Celeste. I am a monster when I turn—uncontrollable. I still might be the one that would be biting you. I can't take that chance."

"Please do it for me," I begged him.

"But I am—I'm taking it for us both."

"Nash, when have I ever asked you to do anything? How can you say no to this? It's only one more month!"

"You are asking me to not be normal anymore. And now that I remember everything—I know what's in my heart. I can't be the one who hurts you."

"I am asking you to do something for me. For once in your life not to leave me just sitting on the sidelines, helping *you*." I was so exasperated with his selfishness. "Uh, Brandon was right. He can do this on his own. I was stupid to think you cared about anything but yourself."

I turned away from Nash and stormed off. I could sense his bewilderment as I left him sitting alone, students staring at him as they walked down the stairs.

TEN

the search

H ow are we going to find these guys?" I asked Brandon
in the parking lot after school.

"You said they were hanging out in the woods near your
house. Let's start there."

I hopped into Brandon's Jeep and he drove me to my
neighborhood. As we got close, I wondered what we'd find.
Would they still be there? And if so, how would they react to
Brandon hunting for them?

Brandon parked the Jeep on the street near the wooded
area and we got out. I pointed to the location where I had
seen Ryder and his gang emerge before. Brandon headed
down the hill to the woods, and I followed close behind. He
stepped in and quickly disappeared. He was walking so fast, I
had trouble keeping up with him. Once inside, he paused. He

glanced around. It seemed like he was using his lycan sense to track their scent.

"Over there—" he said, gesturing to the left.

Brandon started again, walking briskly through the grass and twigs and over fallen branches. I had to jog to keep up with him.

Within a few minutes, Brandon had found their hangout. "Look," he said.

There were three sleeping bags, a cooler, and a filled green garbage bag.

"So they've been sleeping out in the woods?" I said, mortified.

"They've been here for a few days," he said.

Brandon noticed a book on one of the sleeping bags. He bent down and picked it up and flipped through it. "It's a journal," he said.

Then he stood up.

"What is it?" I asked.

"They're coming."

My heart felt like it stopped. I could barely breathe, and I froze in my position. He didn't have time to replace the journal and instead handed it to me. I held on to it as Brandon grabbed me and pulled me behind a tree. We waited as snapping branches and voices were heard coming our way.

We both tried to breathe as quietly as we could.

I couldn't make out their conversation until they reached the campsite, where their jovial mood quickly changed.

"Hey, someone was here," Ryder said.

"Goldilocks?" Leopold asked with a laugh.

"I think someone like us," Ryder said cryptically.

"It could just be a wolf," Hunter said. "They do have them in this town, you know."

"We know," Leopold replied. "But we aren't worried about wolves finding us here."

"My journal is missing," Ryder said.

"I hope you didn't write about our plans in it," Hunter said.

"I'm not stupid—" Ryder shot back. "I just use it for notes."

"Shh," Leopold said. "They might still be here."

They all paused, listening carefully, trying to sense if someone else was in the area.

"I think it might be deer—" Hunter said.

"I don't sense deer. I sense human."

The sound of his footsteps grew louder as he inched our way, ever so slowly approaching the tree we were hiding behind.

"Don't move," Brandon whispered in my ear. "They can't know you are here, too." His soft voice sent goose bumps through me, but they were mixed with feelings of fear.

Brandon suddenly jumped out from behind the tree and faced Ryder head-on.

"Hey—" Ryder shouted.

The others rushed over. I heard scuffling, and I hoped everything was okay.

I tried my best to listen to what was happening.

"What's going on, man?" Leopold charged.

Brandon didn't respond. I could feel the tension of his sudden appearance all the way to the tree that I was hiding behind.

"Hey, I know you—" Ryder said.

"I don't think you do," Brandon said firmly.

"I do. I know I do."

"Yes, it's that dude you checked in the championship game," Hunter said.

"Yes," Ryder said. "Maddox. From Miller's Glen."

"Don't you remember us?" Leopold asked sarcastically.

"How could he forget?" Ryder pressed.

"What are you doing here?" Brandon asked. From Brandon's tense tone I guessed they weren't friends.

"What are *you* doing here?" Hunter asked.

"This is a private community," Brandon said. "Not a campsite."

"What are you, the Housing Authority?" Ryder asked.

His cohorts laughed.

"I've heard you are harassing some girls," Brandon said, his voice still firm. "And I'm here to stop it."

Then Ryder paused. "Maddox. You live around here?"

Brandon didn't answer.

"I thought you were in Miller's Glen," Ryder said.

"I thought you lived in Huntington," Brandon said. It was a neighboring town to both Legend's Run and Miller's Glen.

"We are. We are just visiting. What about you?"

Brandon didn't respond.

"Weird that you'd leave a town where you are the most popular jock," Ryder told him. "It must have been that championship game that you lost. I guess you had to run away from the pain?"

Brandon was the most popular jock in Miller's Glen? I could see how he could be—I always thought he was unrecognized for his handsome good looks here just because he lived on the Westside. It was just like Brandon, so humble and endearing, that he never let on about his popularity back home while he sat alone here at school.

I leaned in a little more but still made sure I remained hidden by the leaves on the tree.

"So, you couldn't take the heat from the community?" he said. "It must have melted the very ice you stood on."

"I don't need to explain to you why I'm here."

"So you live in this posh area, do you?" Ryder asked. "Rich boy doesn't get what he wanted and moves to another town to escape."

Rich boy—I wondered. Brandon never gave me the impression he was a rich kid.

"So you are Mr. Popular in this town, too?" Ryder suggested adamantly. "Playing the part of the young hero. Doesn't seem fitting, though. I guess this town doesn't know about you being a loser."

Brandon didn't answer. I wasn't sure what they were referring to.

"Do you still have the scar?" Ryder asked.

"I should have ended this with you when I had the

chance," Brandon said.

"With a hockey stick? Or fists?"

"I don't need to resort to such tactics," Brandon said.

"Well, we have the trophy," Ryder said.

"And I have my integrity."

"Integrity is overrated," Ryder said. "That can't sit on your shelf or be displayed at your school."

"It's time you leave. You can harass me all you want, but my friends? That's another story."

"You know those girls?" Ryder asked.

Now I really perked up. I scooted a smidge more behind the tree but still safely out of view.

"They were mighty cute," Leopold commented.

"Are they all your girlfriends?" Hunter wondered.

"I think it's time for you to go," Brandon said.

"I think it's time for *you* to go," Ryder said vehemently.

Brandon didn't back down. "You can pack up and move on—or you can stay here, actually. The police in this area don't have much to do. I'm sure they'd love to pick up a few vagrant trespassers."

I wondered what Brandon was up to. The guys were too close for comfort. But if they were moved, who knows where they'd go?

"We came for the Werewolf Fest," Ryder said, not moving. "After that, we'll be gone. In fact, you might even miss us."

"You are interested in werewolves?" Brandon asked.

"It's something in our blood," Hunter said.

"Really?" Brandon said.

"Yes," Ryder said. "Something we feel greatly connected to."

Brandon paused. I could feel the tension he was feeling from where I was standing.

"We won't be here for long," Ryder said. "You don't have to worry about that. We're just here to see the fest and pick up a few things."

"'Pick up a few things?'"

"Yes, some things we can't find in Huntington. And we thought the Werewolf Fest would be a good place to find it."

"You can't stay here," Brandon said firmly. "You'll be kicked out for sure."

"But we are so close to some things we love."

I felt a chill go through me.

"You are in the middle of the suburbs," Brandon said. "That doesn't sound like a great place to camp."

"We happen to like the people here," Ryder said.

"You can't stay here," Brandon reiterated. "I found you. So will others."

"You might be right," Ryder said, resigned. "Now we'll have to find a place that no one knows about. Let's pack up our things."

Leopold and Hunter reluctantly began to roll up their sleeping bags.

"So where are you going?" Brandon wondered.

"You'll never know, will you?" Ryder asked. "And why

does it matter so much to you?"

Brandon didn't answer.

"Why don't you guys stay in a hotel or something?"

"We like the outdoors. Seems natural to us."

"I can point you to some campsites," Brandon said. "Away from the burbs."

"We can find something on our own. Someplace where no one will find us," he said strangely.

"I might know where you can stay."

"Again, we can find something ourselves. We kind of have a sixth sense for such things."

"No, I mean I have a great place to camp. It's behind my guesthouse. There is a huge wooded area there."

"Really?" Ryder wondered skeptically.

"Yes. Just what you are looking for," Brandon confirmed.

"You'd do that for us?" Ryder asked. "Even after that fight at the game? And you'd let me stay at your home? Is this a trick?"

Brandon shrugged his shoulders. "What choice do you have? Get caught by the police or stay on my property and wonder if I'm tricking you?" Then Brandon grabbed the cooler.

"Always the good guy," Hunter said. "Some things never change."

"Change?" Brandon said. "I'm all about change since I moved here."

"Keeping friends close but enemies even closer," Ryder

said, patting Brandon on the back.

"Yes, something like that," Brandon replied.

What was Brandon doing? Inviting these guys to camp out at his house?

They gathered their belongings, and when the others weren't looking, Brandon turned back to me. He held up an imaginary phone to his ear and mouthed, "I'll call you."

I nodded as they made their way out of the woods.

I heard them close the doors to their cars and I began making my own way out, past their former campsite and through some thorny brush. When I saw the Jeep and the car following it leave my community, I stepped out of the woods and headed up the hill toward my house, holding Ryder's journal close to my chest. I couldn't wait to devour it.

I sat on my bed and opened Ryder's journal. It was black leather and slightly worn on the binding and edges. There was a lot of writing in its pages, and he must have reread the last portion of its contents, as the pages seemed to have been turned a lot. The entries were in black marker, and his handwriting was slightly erratic. It seemed appropriate for him.

Day one

I don't know what is happening to me. I've been having such strange dreams ever since that horrible accident last night. I feel so strange, as if I'm living in the woods instead of inside my home. I feel so restless. I don't know what is going on with me.

Then I skipped to the parts where the pages had been turned a lot to get a glimpse of what he was so interested in rereading.

Day fifty-three
Arrived in Legend's Run. We only have a week to find someone. I am hoping we can do this.
Saw a cute girl at convenience store.
Medium-blonde hair. Smile to die for. Pink headband.

Ryder was talking about *me*.

Feisty, in a good way. Beauty that makes the heart race. Sense of good and sweetness. That is something that would be great for someone as tortured as me.

Day fifty-four
Spotted a group of girls outside a fast-food restaurant. One stood out. Heidi is her name. She's so hot I could imagine myself with her. But for the rest of my life? She was very stuck up and reeked of designer perfume.
Still can't get that girl with the pink headband off my mind.
Leopold and Hunter not sure if she is right. But who are they to question me anyway?

The moon is approaching. I can already feel it rage inside me.
When will this end? If I can't be cured, who will love me? The
only way is to find someone sympathetic and loving who would
be able to accept me—and become like me.

That evening, I was trying to do my history homework in my room. But how could I concentrate? The full moon would begin a week from tonight, and not only were Nash and Brandon going to become werewolves, but there was a possibility that Ryder and his gang would, too. And if they were wanting to add girls to their pack, how were we going to stop that from happening? I was trying my best to finish my work, but when I glanced at the presidential portraits on my computer, all I saw were werewolves staring back at me. Then I heard Sinatra sing "Fly Me to the Moon" and I was shaken out of my trance. I grabbed my phone and read the text:

I'm outside.

I jumped out of my chair, hurried downstairs, and opened the front door. I didn't see anyone. "Brandon?" I called.

Then I heard Champ barking at the back door. I shut the front door and flew through the house to the kitchen. I held Champ at bay so he wouldn't run out and opened the door. Brandon was standing on the deck.

"I'm so glad to see you," I said, running to him.

"I'm sorry I had to leave you alone," he said, hugging me. "But you have to understand I couldn't let them know you were there."

"Of course," I agreed.

"And I knew we were so close to your house that you could walk."

"It's okay," I tried to assure him. "You didn't have to drive me the one block."

We both laughed.

He leaned in and kissed me. "I've been waiting all day to do that," he said.

Brandon's kisses were so wonderful; I was so happy when we could get a moment to be together.

He fell into my embrace. I knew I was distracted, but Brandon was the werewolf; he had to deal with the full moon way more than I did. And to top that off, he was taking on the responsibility of getting a cure for Nash and now keeping an eye out on three new werewolves.

"I know you are going through a lot," I said.

Brandon gave me a funny look as if he was so distracted with Ryder that he didn't even have time to process what he was juggling.

"Thanks," he said, rubbing my shoulder. "You always know what to say."

We grabbed hands and sat on the glider. I curled my legs up next to me and scooted as close to Brandon as physically possible. The crickets chirped and lightning bugs flashed around us. I stroked his thick, dark hair as we talked.

"So what happened?" I asked. "Are they really staying with you?"

He nodded. "Yeah. Out back."

"You think that's best?" I wondered. "They are there alone now?"

"My grandparents' house is locked, and so is my guesthouse. There's nothing they can really do in the woods. Besides, I don't have a choice. I have to keep as much an eye out for them as I can. If they are loose in town, who knows where they'll show up, and when? And if they are werewolves . . ."

"You did the right thing. You always do."

"I know it seems weird—Ryder's the last person I want to help out. But having him close to me, I can try to make sure he doesn't bother you again."

I squeezed his hand.

"What was he talking about—losing a game and a fight?"

"Oh, that. He was talking about hockey. I was on the team at my old school in Miller's Glen. We played Huntington in the championship game."

"And what scar?"

"It's gone." He held out his palm. "In fact, I have a new one there."

"He cut your hand?"

"Kind of. It was the final period of the championship game. I was coming in on goal, and he cross-checked me—he came at me with his stick."

"But you didn't hit him—he hit you."

"Right, I blocked the stick with my hand. He was thrown

out of the game, and I was hurt—I had to get stitches. But it was the only way he knew how to win—to have me sitting on the bench."

"He doesn't play fair," I said.

"That's why I thought it was best for me to keep them close, so I can keep an eye out. He's too sneaky." He was quiet for a moment. "That guy. I can't believe he's in Legend's Run. And to think he might be like me?"

"He's not like you—by day or by night," I reassured him.

He leaned his head on my shoulder. For a moment, we just sat quietly, holding hands and listening to the sounds of nature.

We gazed up at the stars, the moon shining down at us.

"It will be full soon," Brandon said, sitting up.

"I know. . . ." I said, facing him.

"I have to figure out so many things before then. But I don't have enough time."

"Brandon, I read Ryder's journal."

Brandon perked up. He smiled as brightly as the moon. "What did you find out?"

"He's looking for a girl to join his gang."

"You were right."

"I want you to see it."

Brandon waited while I left him and returned with the journal.

I opened the book and pointed to one of the entries.

He read it under the floodlight. His expression grew surprised, then angry.

"A girl with a pink headband at the convenience store? That's you."

He flipped through the journal, reading other passages. "He's in love with you."

"He thinks he is. He doesn't even know me."

"He thinks he's coming for you. And I'm letting him stay in my backyard? I should kick him to the curb."

"No—what you did was perfect. It really is the only way."

"When he finds out we are together, he'll try to be with you even more. I have to do something," he thought aloud as he gazed up again at the moon. "Maybe I can convince them to go home before the full moon hits."

"How are you going to be able to do that?"

"I'm not sure." Brandon was thoughtful. "Why wouldn't he just pick someone in Huntington?"

Then I showed him the passage that tied it all together.

The Legend's Run Werewolf Festival. The perfect time to find and take my mate. With everyone acting like werewolves, no one will know that I really am one. I can walk proudly underneath the moon and stars—for one full night—and go unnoticed. It will be that night that I'll find her—and when no one sees, I'll take her as my own.
And her name is Celeste.

Brandon slammed the book shut. He stood up and gripped the book so tightly I thought it was going to break into pieces.

"It's okay," I said, rising, too.

"No, it's not. It's so not okay! I have to stop them from going to the festival." He began pacing.

"But how?"

He stopped. "Maybe tell them I'm a werewolf, too."

"You can't, Brandon. Who knows who they'll tell?"

"I don't know, Celeste. I'm not sure what to do. The full moon is coming, and all I know is I have to do *something*."

I'd never seen Brandon so distraught. I knew he grappled with being a werewolf himself, but he was having a hard time with the knowledge that someone would want to change me.

"What if you go somewhere?" he asked.

"Leave town?"

"Yes." He was excited by his idea. "It's the best solution."

"I can't just go out of town. What would I tell my parents?"

"We could think of something."

"Where would I go?" I wondered. "And how would I get there?"

"We can work out all those details."

"I can't miss school. I have so many tests next week."

"You can make them up. This is more important. My grandma has a sister in Madison you can stay with. I'll get you a bus ticket."

"Brandon," I began. "I really appreciate it, but I'm not

going to leave. I'm going to face this thing with you. I'm not leaving you alone."

"Me?" he said. "You are worried about me?" He stroked the top of my hair and kissed my forehead. "You are always thinking of others. Can't you just once think of yourself?"

"No, I'm not going to just run off and leave you here to deal with these guys by yourself." I stood firm.

He gazed at me proudly. Then he felt he needed to defend his own pride.

"I didn't run away, either," he said. "From Miller's Glen."

"I know that."

"You heard Ryder say I did. But that's not what happened."

"I know," I said. "It was because of your father. He went to Europe, and you couldn't stay there yourself. Anyway, it was just a game," I continued. "That's all."

"But this isn't. This is so much more."

I took his hand and led him back to the glider. "So, you were like Nash at your old school? The popular jock?"

"Yes, even after we lost. We were upset—but most thought I was even cooler than I'd been before."

"Then how did you deal with it here? Sitting alone, having no friends?"

"It was hard. Really. But there was something about it that was really good for me: I got to see a side of life I didn't see when I was home. Everything in my old life was about sports and parties. And here, I got to spend more time outdoors. But mostly, I got to meet the one person who mattered to me more than anyone I'd ever met before."

"You are so sweet," I said, giving him a squeeze. "I am so glad you came to Legend's Run."

"Me, too," he said. "However, I'm not so happy Ryder came as well."

"I double that," I said.

"But know this," Brandon said. "You don't have to worry. This is one game against Ryder that I *will* win."

ELEVEN

sisterly advice

I stewed over reading more of Ryder's journal. Normally I wasn't one to snoop—or read another person's intimate writings without their consent—but in this case it was imperative. It was the key to Ryder's actions, and since my friends and I could possibly be in danger, I was doing more harm by not reading it than by reading it.

I sat at my desk and opened the journal again.

Day thirty-two

I hate who I've become. Destined for a life of solitude. Is this really me? What has happened?

If Leopold and Hunter hadn't teased those wolves at the animal sanctuary, none of this would have happened. We were lucky they didn't kill us. It was stupid to sneak in after

dark—and nothing goes right on a dare.
But my arm didn't heal well—and theirs didn't, either.
We all had fevers and bizarre dreams. We are all freaked
out—afraid to admit to what really transpired and chalked
it up to delusions from our fevers. But when I saw Hunter
and Leopold change last night, I knew I was going to follow.
Though I don't remember what happened next, I know from
watching them that I, too, turned into a monster. And this
isn't going away. I don't know what to do anymore but run.

Ryder was experiencing the same anguish that Brandon and Nash had gone through. He was rough around the edges—there was no doubt about that—but this must have pushed him over the line. The whole lycan condition was fraught with torment, anxiety, and isolation. Even though his friends also experienced it, he was still lonely and scared like Brandon and Nash had been. For some reason Brandon handled it the best. It magnified his already good qualities. It made him stronger, and even more handsome. But that didn't mean that it was all glory for him. He had to deal with it just like the others—and that caused strain in his life. And as for Nash, it was wrecking him. I felt awful that any of these guys had to go through this horrible condition when it was tough enough already to deal with the normal challenges of high school.

I had compassion for Ryder—even though he was making it a point to bother me and my friends. He was going about dealing with his condition in the wrong way, but now that I'd read his thoughts, I wasn't sure he knew how to do it any differently.

As I reread the journal entries, I couldn't help but wonder about his attraction to me. Nash was the first major crush I'd had, and Brandon was my first—and only—true love. But Ryder stood somewhere else. For some reason, he was drawn to me—but I couldn't figure out why. He was the complete opposite of Brandon, really—and of me and my family. His style was very rough and edgy and he appeared to be dangerous. I couldn't stop thinking about him. And then I realized my fear had turned into fascination.

It had been a while since Juliette had come home from school. She popped in the following day, Saturday, to get some extra cash and more spring clothes.

"It's wonderful to see you," my mom said to her.

Our house was so much quieter when Juliette was away. And though I loved the solitude and being the only daughter for a change, there was a tiny part of me that did miss my big sister.

I sat on her bed. Her room was still the same as she left it. Mom and Dad were hoping to use her room as an office, but they wound up leaving it intact until she decided what she'd do after college. I thought it was more to do with my mom not wanting to let her daughter go completely.

"So how is school?" I asked.

"Love it. It's so much fun. What about you? Mom tells me you have a boyfriend. And it's not Nash."

I blushed.

"Is this the hot guy you were talking to me about last time when I came into town?"

"Yes."

"So what's he like?"

"He's everything I could imagine wanting. He's strong and handsome and funny and kind."

"Does he have a brother?"

"No," I answered with a laugh.

"So, what else?"

"There's this one other guy. I don't like him or anything. But he follows me, and he's really different. I wonder what it would be like . . ."

"So you have a crush. Big deal."

"You think so?"

"Hello. It's normal to find other guys attractive."

"But why him? He's rude and weird and has tatts all over."

"Sounds like my kind of man. Is he hot?"

I nodded.

"You know what I think? It's because he's different—the opposite of you and everything you want. Brandon is what you really desire, and this guy is someone you'd never see yourself with. So that makes him cool, too. The unknown, an adventure. Maybe it's about disclosing a rebellious and dangerous part of yourself that you find thrilling." She got a mischievous glint in her eye. "Have you kissed him?"

"No!"

"But you want to."

"No!" I said again. "I just don't know why I think about him."

"Because you have a mind."

"So it's not cheating?"

"You have to do a lot more than think about a guy to be a cheater," Juliette reassured me.

I gave her a squeeze.

"You are such a dork sometimes. I can't believe you are my sister," Juliette teased.

But I still felt odd that I was thinking about Ryder.

TWELVE

canoe trip

think we need a break from everything," Brandon said on the phone to me before I went to bed. "I have just the idea for a little R & R tomorrow."

I was in great need of rest and relaxation, and it would be wonderful for Brandon and me to have some free time spent together, forgetting all about Ryder, Nash, and the effects of the full moon.

"Pack a swimsuit and sunscreen," he said, "and I'll pick you up around nine thirty."

At nine fifteen, I was anxiously waiting outside my house for Brandon. I wore a bikini under a pair of hiking shorts and a light blue tank top. He pulled into my driveway at nine thirty, a canoe tied to the top of his Jeep. I got into his SUV, and we drove down the twisty and hilly back roads of the

Westside. His grandmother had packed sandwiches, fruit, and drinks in a cooler. The windows were rolled down, and the music was turned up. We sang along to our favorite songs as we headed over a two-lane bridge. I gazed out—endless trees and a high river. I was having the best time already. We continued on and passed open fields, farms, and horse stables. We came around a corner to the bank of the river and parked in a gravel parking lot. There were a handful of people already there—and kids running around with oars and life jackets.

I felt funny being in my bathing suit in front of Brandon, so I just took off my T-shirt and kept my shorts on. I wasn't tan yet—and I knew I needn't be—but I did feel self-conscious. The life jacket was lumpy, making me feel even more unattractive than I felt before.

"You sit in front," he said with the confidence of a navy commander.

I hopped in, and he pushed the canoe against the sandy embankment and into the river as he jumped in behind me.

I paddled a bit while he steered. Our surroundings were beautiful. Within a few minutes we were in the middle of the river, trees and summerhouses lining the sides. There was no sign of normal traffic even though the roads weren't too far away from us.

I leaned back and closed my eyes. The sun's rays felt amazing against my skin. The smell of the river was fresh from the beginning of spring. In a few months, this same river would be hot and muggy, and mosquitoes would be pecking at us. It was a perfect time to canoe.

"I'd love to do this every day," I said. "Thank you for bringing me! I can't imagine Ivy on the river."

"I can't, either."

"Abby—she'd love it. But we get so busy with school and things, we don't think of doing fun stuff like this."

"Things seem different since I've changed. I feel the need to be outside as much as possible. I loved the outdoors before—but now I can't seem to get enough of it. I almost feel claustrophobic in school or in my room at home. Here you can feel so free."

"There's nothing out here to bother us." Just then I glanced up. I thought I saw red and blond hair peeking out from one of the trees. "Is that—"

Brandon looked in the direction I had, but the guys were gone.

"What?"

"I thought I saw Leopold—or Hunter."

"They are supposed to be at my house, chopping wood. I offered to pay them, and they accepted. I knew that would keep them busy for a while and help me out at the same time. They can't be a danger to us now."

"I know," I said. But did I really? Why couldn't they be? Were they only dangerous if they were in werewolf form? I didn't feel like we were so alone anymore.

Brandon tried to distract me. "Cool, there's a rope swing

on that tree. You want to go for a swing?"

"I couldn't possibly."

"Sure you can. I'll go, too."

We beached the canoe and watched as several kids, one by one, climbed up the tree, then the branch, grabbed the rope, and swung into the water.

It looked like great fun. Only when it was our turn, it wasn't as easy as it appeared. I grabbed the branch and tried my best to keep my footing. Brandon was right behind me, and he laughed at me as I squealed several times.

"I'm doing my best," I said.

"You're almost there," he encouraged.

The water seemed farther away than it had when we were looking up at the rope. The other kids were back in their boats but were watching me.

"You can do it," one shouted.

I grabbed the rope, and it shook in my hands.

If Brandon wasn't standing behind me, I would have surely turned around and climbed down. But he smiled as if he was so proud of me, and I didn't want to disappoint him.

I took a deep breath and jumped off the branch. I only knew that I was screaming with delight as I swung in the air, and before I knew it I was smacking my body into the water. It wasn't an Olympic feat by any stretch of the imagination. I treaded water while I watched Brandon take my place.

Brandon waved and quickly swung in after me. He was much more graceful. I swam over to him.

"That was so much fun," I said. Then I giggled. "I was afraid I'd lose my top!"

"I was kind of hoping you would," he teased.

"Get out—" I toyed with him. I swam away and headed for the embankment.

When I glanced up, I saw Ryder leaning against a tree.

I gasped. I turned to Brandon, who was still swimming toward me.

"Brandon," I whispered. But he was still too far away.

I turned back to Ryder, who was still standing there. This time he gave me a wink. I cringed inside. I didn't know what he was up to, but I felt like he was invading our space and good time.

All at once, I felt someone behind me, pinching my sides.

I screamed.

I turned around to find Brandon laughing.

"Why are you so nervous?" he said. "Who did you think it was?"

"Ryder is over there," I whispered to him so he could hear.

He glanced around.

"Where?"

"By the tree."

"I don't see him."

I turned around casually. Ryder had gone.

I headed farther up the embankment and searched as much as I could from where I was.

"He was right over there—" I said, pointing.

"It's okay. Even if they are here—what does it matter?"

"Haven't you seen those movies? Someone following people on the river? There are tons of them."

"It's okay," he said, pulling me close. "If he is here, he's doing exactly what he wants—getting under your skin. The best thing is to ignore him. Have a good time. That's the best payback."

I nodded my head. "You're right."

Brandon never asked for anything. And this was one opportunity that he could just be himself. I shouldn't let anyone get in the way. Even if it was upsetting to me.

I did see Ryder again, but I didn't say anything to Brandon. I kept my cool and talked really loudly about how good of a time I was having.

"It's okay," Brandon whispered. "I sense him spying on us. But we don't have to worry about it. This is our time together."

He leaned in to me and kissed me long. His luscious lips sent tingles racing along my damp skin.

We ate our sandwiches and cuddled in the canoe. The atmosphere, sounds, and scenery were breathtaking, and being in the wilderness with my now-human but soon-to-be-werewolf boyfriend was magical. I wasn't going to let another lycan spoil these precious moments anymore.

After some more relaxing, we stretched out and then packed up our lunches and resumed our trip.

As we made our way down the river, there were a few rapids, and with Brandon's guidance we made our way through them. It was exhilarating; I felt a rush paddling through them. "I wish there were more," I said.

Before I knew it, we'd come to the pickup point.

"It's over already?"

"Next we can do the five-mile trip."

"My arms are sore from paddling, I have to admit."

We got into the van, and Brandon massaged my arms.

I leaned my head on his shoulder as I looked back. I saw Ryder standing at the edge of the embankment—staring up at me. This time I bravely looked back at him and waved. He was lucky the gesture was a polite one.

The full moon was fast approaching, and I knew changes would soon be happening. I was just hoping I wouldn't be one of those to change.

THIRTEEN

a few good friends

A few days later, I was becoming anxious again with the full moon fast approaching. I caught up to my friends in the girls' locker room. Abby was getting ready for volleyball practice, and Ivy was using Abby's locker mirror to touch up her makeup.

"I have to ask you something, and I know you guys will think I'm crazy," I said.

A few of the other athletes shut their lockers and headed out.

"Sure," Abby said. "But you'll have to make it quick."

"On Saturday night," I began in an ultra-happy tone, "how about you guys come to my house for movies?"

"That's the day of the Werewolf Fest," Abby said.

"Yes, can you make it another day?" Ivy asked, puckering her lips in the mirror.

"No," I replied gently. "It has to be that night."

"Well, we are going to the fest. Aren't you?" Abby asked.

"I was going to. But I thought it might be fun to have a girls' night instead." I tried to be lighthearted about the matter.

"On the biggest night of the year besides prom?" Abby said.

"The Werewolf Fest only happens every ten years." Ivy turned to me.

Even though I'd read in Ryder's journal that he was after me, I knew the other guys were also looking for girlfriends. I wanted to make sure my friends were not in harm's way, too. "No way am I missing it," Abby insisted.

"You can't go," I said with a forceful whisper. "It could be dangerous."

"Dangerous?" Abby laughed. "Get out."

"Those guys who have been bugging us are going to be there," I protested.

"So?" Ivy asked. "What's the big deal?"

"What if they bother us again?" I asked.

"Jake and Dylan will kick their—"

"What if they can't?" I interrupted. "What if these guys are stronger?"

"Than Jake, Dylan, Nash, *and* Brandon?" Ivy said. "I don't think so."

"And me," Abby said. "I can defend us, too."

"I'm not going to let them keep me home," Ivy said.

"I think they are after me, and maybe you, too," I

whispered. "And I think we'll be safer if we stay home that night."

"You are kidding," Ivy said.

"No, I'm not. I got Ryder's journal."

"Where did you find that?" Abby asked, interested.

"They were camping out over by the woods in my neighborhood," I said.

"Where you live?" Abby wondered.

"Yes, that's what I was trying to tell you," I replied. "Only Brandon convinced them to go to his house to camp out—so he could watch them."

"That was nice of him, but really," Ivy went on, "they didn't do anything wrong."

"You saw them following us at the mall," I said. "And then that time they snuck up on me when I was walking Champ? Now they show up camping near my house?"

"Yes, but that was all," Ivy replied.

"Fortunately," I said, still pressing my point. "But I think they are planning something for the festival."

"I'm not saying we should marry them," Ivy said. "I'm just saying that I'm not going to let them stop me from going to the best event in our town's history."

I took a deep breath as Abby shut her locker and pulled up her volleyball socks. "You just have to believe me," I pleaded. "It's for our own good."

"I think you are just being overprotective." Ivy patted me on the back. "Everyone will be there. Nothing will happen to any of us."

"It will be a full moon," I warned them.

"I know, that's the point," Ivy said. "It will be so cool."

"It won't be cool. They aren't like us."

"Thank goodness. I wouldn't look good covered in tattoos." Ivy giggled.

"I think you would," Abby thought aloud. "You could cover yourself in designer labels," she teased.

"I'm serious," I said. "They are *really* different. More different than you can imagine."

"What are you getting at?" Ivy said. "If you are asking us to miss the fest, there must be a good reason. So just come out and say it."

I leaned in and spoke softly. "Because they are werewolves," I said.

My friends stared at me for a few seconds.

"What?" Ivy asked.

"You are crazy!" Abby said.

"I knew you'd think so."

They both laughed. "Is that all? That they are werewolves?" Ivy asked. "I thought you were going to say convicts or something."

"Yes, or runaways from an asylum," Abby said.

"So you believe me?" I wondered.

Abby began to leave, and we followed.

"I believe you are afraid of werewolves, but I don't believe in them," Ivy said. "There are tons of underground weirdos like that. I've seen shows on TV about that."

"They think they are werewolves because they want to

scare girls," Abby told us. "It's the oldest trick in the book. Just like on Halloween, guys dress up as monsters. They are just getting in the spirit of the fest. Like Trekkies. Only these guys aren't nerds."

"They're wackos!" Ivy added.

They both laughed.

I wasn't getting the response I wanted from my friends. I knew they wouldn't believe me, but I had to try. "Let's just say they might be taking it too far."

"Like a certain someone who wears a Superman cape," Ivy said, "but doesn't want to take it off?"

"Something like that," I said.

"So they are going to howl at the moon?" Ivy asked.

"They want to turn us into werewolves."

They both laughed again.

"I'll already be one," Abby said. "I'm dressing up."

"Have I ever lied to you before?" I finally asked them when we reached the gym.

"Uh . . . no," Ivy admitted.

"Not to me," Abby said. "You didn't lie to us about dating Brandon. You just withheld the information. That's not a lie."

"Have I ever tried to get in the way of your fun?" I asked.

They paused and both shook their heads.

"You have to believe me. This once," I said. "I never ask anything from you guys."

"But you are asking us to miss the best event in this town's history because of three pranksters," Ivy whined.

The coach blew her whistle.

"I gotta run," Abby said.

I grabbed her jersey. "I'm your best friend. I never ask anything of you guys. And once, I ask something of you both—for your own good—and you ignore me. Fine. I warned you, like Dr. Meadows warned me. But I didn't listen and so many things happened."

"Don't go all 'crazy girl' on us," Ivy said.

"Like when Dr. Meadows warned you and then those wolves stalked you in the snow?" Abby asked.

I nodded.

"All right," Abby relented as I let go. "I'll come over."

"You will?" I asked eagerly.

She high-fived me and ran off to join her teammates.

I was left standing with Ivy.

"I guess I'll come, too," she said resignedly.

I put my arm around her shoulder. "You are the greatest!"

"Yes, but if we miss anyone else being bitten, then I'm really going to be mad," Ivy teased.

I was relieved. "You won't regret this."

"You better have some amazing movies and piping-hot pizza for us," Ivy said.

"I promise."

"We are all set," I told Brandon when I saw him later that day at Willow Park. We decided to meet by the lake—so we could be alone and talk. "Ivy and Abby have agreed to come to my house for a girls' night. They can't bother us if we are at home, right? We have a security system, and I'll keep all the lights on. If Ryder and his crew can't hide under the cloak of darkness and other costumed werewolves, then his plan is blown. Ivy and Abby can stay the night, and in the morning the full moon won't be an issue."

"You are a good friend to them," Brandon said.

"They think I'm nuts." I couldn't help but laugh. "Here they were the ones dragging me to Dr. Meadows, and now I'm the one talking about sixth senses."

"I do have some good news," he said.

"Good news? Tell me."

"My dad called and said he's sent another vial of werewolf antidote. Nash will be able to take the one I already have. And I had a thought about the other vial."

"You'll take it the following night?"

"No—Ryder will first. My dad said this batch is really potent. It will work by taking just one sip. 'There will be no excuses this time for you not to take it,' he said. But if we cure Ryder, then our problems will be just about over. And we'll have enough serum left for me."

"And Leopold and Hunter?" I asked.

"Perhaps there will be enough for all of us . . ." he said, hopeful.

"That's awesome. You'll tell Ryder about it?"

"No, I can't. I can't let him know that I know about his condition."

"But I think he'd be okay with it since you have a cure. I read his journal. He's not happy being a werewolf."

"And you think I am?" he asked.

"I didn't say that," I said.

"I know. I'm just on edge."

I held him close. "It's okay. So much is going on. The fest. Ryder. Nash. We never even get a chance to talk about what you are going through."

We sat down on a nearby bench.

"We haven't had time for anything else," Brandon said. "And now I'm worried about the full moon—I can't imagine what Ryder will be like. And all I think about is making sure you are okay."

"I will be—we will be." I tried to reassure him, even though I wasn't sure myself.

"Saturday night is the fest," he said. "Then, after that, hopefully they will leave and go back to Huntington."

"And everything will be back to normal," I said, hoping it was true.

"I've honestly forgotten what normal is," Brandon said.

FOURTEEN

the brave one

Nash was stoked all day before the first night of the full moon. I knew that he'd be going to Brandon's for the cure as soon as the sun began to set. He acted like they were best buddies at lunch and the rest of the day at school.

"Please, can't you wait one more day?" I asked after final bell. I still worried that Ryder and his guys would cause trouble and Brandon would need Nash's help in the werewolf department.

He slapped me on the back. "You're so cute with your questions. I'm off for dinner, then catching up to Brandon at his house at dusk. You can kiss my werewolf lips good-bye," he said, puckering up.

I ignored him as I had since we stopped dating. I was incensed that he was so gleeful about taking the serum when there were other potentially dangerous werewolves in our town. I left him standing alone as I, frustrated, slipped away into the crowd of students.

I was waiting with Brandon outside his guesthouse when Nash's BMW pulled into the driveway. Brandon held the serum as Nash hopped out of the car and headed for us. I'd never seen him so happy as he sauntered up to us. But as the sun set behind us, I could see the fear rising in Nash. Perhaps it *was* too much to ask for him to wait to be cured of his condition—even for one more day.

"Here—" Brandon said, handing the serum to Nash. "You'll have to take it after you change. And good luck."

"That's it?"

"Those are the only instructions my father gave me."

"What if he loses control after he's turned and can't take it?" I asked.

"I won't lose control," Nash assured me. "Now that I remember everything, I'll remember why I have it."

"And I'll be here," I said, offering my support. "I'll remind you."

"I'll come back as soon as I change, in case you need my help," Brandon said.

"I really appreciate this, guys. More than you'll ever know," Nash said sincerely. "And I hope Dr. Meadows was right when she talked about a cure. She said, 'When the opportunity is revealed to you, the answer is yes. Take it. You will be normal again.'" Nash was excited about the possibility of being cured, and Dr. Meadows's prediction gave him some comfort. But there still was a risk, and he fidgeted anxiously.

The sun completely set and the full moon glowed behind us.

Nash started to breathe heavily. He lurched away from me and leaned against a tree.

When I turned back to Brandon, he had already disappeared.

"Get away from me," Nash said. Suddenly his eyes turned blue gray. He held the serum in his shaking hand. I was afraid he'd drop it and spill its entire contents.

Against his wishes, I crept close to him.

His hair was now long over his shoulders. He glanced away from me as I took the vial of serum from his now finely haired hand.

He stood in full werewolf form. He turned back to me with lonely eyes. "I know what's happening to me, Celeste. And I hate every minute of this. Please. Let me have that!"

I held the serum in my hand.

"Please," he said. And though he could pounce on me and rip it from my hands easily, he didn't. He waited for me to decide.

I couldn't deny him what he wanted—what he truly needed. I held out the serum to him.

His fangs appeared golden in the moonlight. He reached for it and examined the vial.

He gulped it down as if he were a starving man finding food.

When he finished, we both looked at each other,

wondering what would happen next. But nothing did. I was concerned, and Nash was enraged. He howled fiercely and I covered my ears.

Brandon, in his lycan form, stepped out from behind a tree and raced over to protect me. He was breathing heavily, too.

Then the hair on Nash's chest began to disappear. His wild beard became shorter before, all at once, it was gone. His eyes went back to their natural color.

Nash smiled like he'd won the Heisman Trophy.

There was a bit of sadness emanating from Brandon as he stood as the lone werewolf.

Nash hurried over to me and gave me an excited hug, swinging me around with delight.

"I won't be a werewolf anymore!" he shouted.

I'd never seen him so relieved and happy.

Tears welled in his eyes. He went over to Brandon. "I have to thank you, man. You really saved my life."

Brandon seemed pleased at Nash's words. He gave Nash a brilliant smile, his fangs flashing in the moonlight. Then it hit us all: Nash was cured and Brandon was not.

"I can't leave you here," Nash whispered to me. "He is a werewolf, you know."

"Yes you can," I said loudly enough for all to hear.

Brandon nodded his head.

"He's not going to hurt me," I said, defending him. "He never has."

"You're not going to hurt *me*—are you?" Nash asked.

"You're not mad that I'm normal and you're—"

"Perhaps it's time for you to go," I said.

Nash backed up, and I took Brandon's hand and leaned against him.

As my werewolf boyfriend held me, Nash took off for his car. When he reached it, he paused.

We heard a howling coming from deep within the woods. It was followed by another one, and still another one.

Brandon perked up.

"I have to go find them."

"I'll go, too."

"No, you have to go home," he stated adamantly.

"I want to see them as well. I've seen you and Nash. I can deal with them."

There were several distant howls again.

"Who knows what they are up to?" Brandon wondered. "I have to go."

But I wasn't about to leave his side. "I'm coming, too, Brandon."

I tried to run alongside Brandon, but he was faster, and he could see his path before him where I was blinded by the darkness.

I fell behind, and I stumbled. I hoped I hadn't twisted my ankle.

Brandon stopped and came back for me. "See?" he said. "This is no place for you to be."

"Wherever you are is the place I'm supposed to be," I said, rubbing my ankle.

"Are you okay?" He guided me to a thick, broken tree branch where I sat down. He lifted my leg and checked my ankle.

"I'll take you home."

"No, I'm okay. Really."

"Are you sure?"

I nodded. I rose, but then hobbled. My ankle was sore. I could walk on it but not run.

The sounds of the howling came closer.

"Go on," I said.

"Are you crazy? I'm not leaving you here. Who knows what they'll do."

He scooped me up easily, as if I were a small child, and hoisted me on his back. I wrapped my arms around his neck and hulky chest, his long hair draping over them. He ran through the woods as the howling followed close behind.

Before I knew it, we were racing down the hilltop and heading toward my car. He opened the door and slid me inside.

Brandon hurried around to the driver's side and hopped in. I locked the doors and handed him my keys.

I could see the outlines of three figures with long hair standing on the hilltop.

Brandon drove me home safely and walked me to my door. I kissed him long and held him tightly. There was no place I felt more secure than in his presence, especially when I was nestled against him. He was truly impressive under a waxing or waning moon—but under a full moon he was the hottest werewolf I'd ever known. I didn't want to let go and be away from him even for a minute, but I knew our eventful evening had come to an end. I unlocked my front door and opened it and when I turned around he had already disappeared into the night.

The following day, it was Saturday, the day of the Werewolf Fest. I was on my way to meet Ivy and Abby at the coffee shop when I saw a shaggy blond and a fiery redhead lurking by Dee's Restaurant a few shops over.

They were fidgety and eyeing other's food through the window.

I crept over to them, not knowing how they'd respond to me—or me to them. They seemed sincerely hungry.

"I thought you were at Brandon's," I said.

"Uh . . . we were," Leopold said.

"What are you guys doing hanging out here?" I asked.

"Just getting some air," Hunter replied.

"Where is Ryder?" I wondered aloud.

"He's out somewhere," Leopold replied.

"By himself?"

"He's a big boy," Hunter said.

"Well, why don't you go inside and eat instead of drooling outside?"

They just hung outside instead of going in.

"You don't have any money," I said. Often, I'd given

money to the homeless in our area, and though these two didn't look as down and out, they did seem like they hadn't eaten in days. And if they were truly werewolves, their hunger was more significant than most.

"I thought Brandon was paying you to work."

"He was, but Ryder took it," Leopold lamented, embarrassed.

I opened the door. "C'mon," I said.

They followed me into the restaurant.

"You don't have to do this," Leopold said.

"How else are you going to eat? Table for three," I said.

They eyed the menu as if they hadn't eaten in days.

"Get whatever you like," I said.

"You don't have to do this," Leopold repeated.

"It's okay."

They each ordered a few sandwiches as the waiter looked at them.

"Nothing for me," I said.

"We're sharing," Hunter said as if apologizing for their huge order.

"I thought Brandon and his grandmother were giving you meals," I said.

"They were . . ." Hunter said.

"He just stopped? That doesn't make any sense. Brandon is gracious, not cruel."

"He takes all the food," Leopold finally admitted.

"Brandon does?" I asked, shocked.

Hunter shook his head.

"Oh, Ryder. I should have known." This time I shook my head.

The waiter brought over two large sodas while I texted my friends. They were running late, so I took the opportunity to pump Ryder's friends for information.

"So, are you excited about the Werewolf Fest?" I asked.

"Yes," Leopold said. "It will be a blast."

"Why are you both so interested in werewolves?" I questioned.

"Same reason everyone else is," Hunter replied.

"But you don't live in Legend's Run. Huntington doesn't have a werewolf legend, does it?" I pressed.

"It does, but it's not as known."

"Really?" I wasn't as surprised as I should have been.

"Yes, it's not like you guys own werewolves or anything," Hunter said.

"Be nice," Leopold said.

"I mean the legend thing." Hunter sighed. "It happened in Huntington, too."

"What happened?"

"Werewolves. Apparently your Legend's Run werewolf— or werewolves—made his way to Huntington."

"So, that is why you are interested?" I asked. "Because of one of Huntington's historical residents?"

"It is still happening," Hunter said quietly.

"Ssh!" Leopold said.

Just then the waiter brought their several plates of food. The guys immediately began wolfing down their meals.

"Maybe it isn't such a good idea that you guys are in town," I said. "Just because Ryder wants to be here doesn't mean you both have to be as well."

They both chewed their food and gulped their sodas.

"I know he's bent on finding . . . girlfriends," I said.

They continued eating and didn't respond.

"I just don't want trouble for you," I continued.

"You mean for you?" Hunter corrected.

"Shh," Leopold scolded his friend.

"For any of us," I shot back.

My phone buzzed with a text from Ivy informing me they had arrived at the coffee shop a few doors down.

I picked up the check and looked at it. I dug in my purse and got out enough money for the bill and the tip. I placed it on top of the check.

Leopold grabbed my hand.

"Thank you," he said sincerely. "I guess I know why he likes you."

I felt awkward and blushed slightly. "You don't have to tell him about this," I said as I rose.

"Trust me," Hunter said. "He'll know. He knows everything."

I felt a sudden chill go through me as I headed out of the restaurant.

FIFTEEN

werewolf fest

I was heading outside to walk Champ when I spotted Nash sauntering up my driveway.

"Hey, Celeste," he said.

"Oh . . . hi," I said.

"I really have to thank you and Brandon for what you both have done," he said. "You know, he really is like you—generous."

I half smiled. I was pleased that Nash was so appreciative about Brandon and recognized the wonderful traits I saw.

"But—I'm also sorry. I was so obsessed with becoming cured, I couldn't see beyond that. What it really meant for you—Brandon—the town. I guess I should have tried to help."

"There's nothing you can do about it now," I said.

"Well, at least we know the cure works. No side effects.

All we have to do is have Brandon take it," he said.

"There are other werewolves in town. I told you. Brandon won't take the serum."

"What are you talking about? He has to."

"You know what I'm talking about. I already told you this. Tonight at the fest. Ryder and his friends are planning to try to convert me."

Nash groaned. "What did I do? I should have waited like you asked."

"I understand why you did that. I'm not sure what I would have done."

"I know what you would have done," Nash said. "You would have waited another day just because I asked you to. And because it might have been the right thing to do. That's who you are. But I'm not like you, am I?"

"It was a difficult choice," I said.

"It was right there in front of me. I didn't want to be a werewolf. Not even for one more night. That's all I was thinking about."

"I understand."

"But I can help you out now. I am still strong and can protect you and Ivy and Abby."

"That's okay," I said. "We are going to stay at my house tonight. And those guys think we'll be at the fest, so they'll never know where we really are."

"I'll come over, too. I'll be your bodyguard."

"You don't have to do that," I said. But it did sound like a good idea to have someone with us.

"I insist. It's the least I can do."

"So Brandon will be a werewolf alone—trying to ward off those guys, and you'll come to my house and watch movies? No, I'd rather you keep an eye out at the fest, just in case Brandon needs help."

"Are you sure?" he asked.

"Yes, and maybe you could bring Jake and Dylan, too. We might need the extra muscle."

"I am still so surprised you aren't going to the festival tonight," my mom said when she got home from work. I was straightening up the family room and double-checking that we had enough snacks for the evening.

"We're not into werewolves," I told her.

"But they'll be showing movies, and people will be dressing up in costumes. I would think you'd want to do it, if only to see everyone in town. Besides, when we took you and your sister last time it came around, you loved it."

"I was seven," I said, putting a stack of movies next to the TV. But the truth was, I did love it then, and I knew I would have loved it this time, too. If I didn't think we were in serious danger, I would be having the time of my life. Not only would I be hanging out with my friends, watching scary werewolf movies and eating such treats as bloodred licorice and French-fried fangs, but Brandon would be able to be in front of everyone in his lycan form and they'd just think he was dressing for the festival. I did feel awful missing the best event in this town in ten years. I'd have to wait until I was twenty-seven to attend the next one. However, I knew I was doing the right thing.

It was after eight. Ivy and Abby still hadn't shown up. I was starting to get worried. Had Ryder already gotten to them? I texted Ivy.

I waited a few minutes until she texted back.

With Jake at the fest. Sorry. We just got here. He wanted to enter the contest. PDHM.

Please Don't Hate Me? My best friends stood me up—and now I was going to be all alone. I'm sure I'd be safe at home—but what if I wasn't?

I had to go now, too. Fuming, I rushed to put on my Red Riding Hood outfit from Halloween. Who knew, but it might also protect me from Ryder finding me. I grabbed my purse and keys and jumped into my car and headed straight for the Werewolf Festival.

There was a lot of traffic as I approached downtown—the location of the festival. Everything was decorated with balloons, and I could already see werewolves of all shapes and sizes walking up and down the street.

The last time I attended the fest, I was seven, and I remembered sitting out on the lawn with my family. Even Juliette enjoyed it. But now I was approaching the fest on my own, trying to find my own real werewolf. All kinds of werewolves roamed the street—masked ones, painted ones, cartoon ones.

Food and souvenir vendors lined the street, and a huge white tent was in the middle park area. The main street was closed to traffic, but I could see from where I was that all spaces in view were occupied. If I couldn't find a parking place, I'd be stuck driving around all night and wouldn't be able to catch up to my friends.

I called Brandon as I sat in traffic.

"Where are you?" I asked.

"I'm at the fest. Are you having fun with your friends?"

"What friends? They stood me up. They are here somewhere."

"Here?" he asked. "Where are you?"

"Trying to find a parking space."

"I'm by Sixth Street. There are some empty lots."

I passed a guy who was parking and drove toward Sixth Street. I saw Brandon on the corner, pointing to a vacant space.

I pulled in, and Brandon kindly gave the lot owner money.

I took a moment to catch my breath. Brandon was standing in the lot, barefoot and shirtless, his chest heaving like he'd run a race. His hair was wildly long and untamed. I ran up to him and kissed him.

"What happened to your plans?" he asked when we drew apart.

"They didn't come," I said, disappointed. "So I'm here."

"Well, I guess we tried," he said. "I'll just have to keep an eye out for you. You promise not to leave my side?"

"I wouldn't want to be anywhere else," I said.

We walked a few blocks to the entrance of the festival.

I called Ivy, but she didn't answer.

Then I called Abby. She didn't answer her phone, either.

"How am I going to find them?" I asked.

The whole town was out for the festival.

It really was a splendid event, if I hadn't been so distracted by everything.

"Do you know where Ryder is?" I asked.

"I tried to get him to meet me—so we could go together. But he ditched me, too."

"We've both been stood up tonight," I said.

"I'd much rather be with you," he said. "Under the full moonlight. It really agrees with you. You are so beautiful."

I couldn't help but blush and leaned into him, giving him a tight squeeze.

Just then we heard screaming.

"What's that?" I asked.

Fear shot through me. All I could think of was Ivy and Abby being attacked by Ryder and his friends.

We raced in the direction of the scream and when we arrived, we saw that it was only a few girls riding a mini–roller coaster.

"I guess I'm a bit jumpy," I said.

I heard someone call my name from behind me.

"Celeste!"

I turned around. It was Ivy, Abby, Dylan, and Jake. Dylan and Jake were dressed haphazardly as werewolves, with drawn-on beards and plastic fangs. And Ivy and Abby both were pretty as damsels in distress, with torn outfits.

"We are so sorry," Ivy said.

"Will you forgive us?" Abby asked.

I was angry. How could I not be? But I had other things to worry about now.

"Finally, we are all here," I said. "We need to stick together. There is safety in numbers."

"Afraid a werewolf will get us?" Ivy asked, giggling.

"Yes," I said truthfully.

"Well, Brandon can save us," Abby said. "He's always doing that—and tonight he even looks like a werewolf."

"The costume contest is going to be in an hour," Abby said. "How about having some fun until then?!"

We all headed for the rides, where we bought tickets and rode the Octopus, the Scrambler, and finally the Ferris wheel. When Brandon and I were at the top, the ride stopped to let another group on. We looked around from our bird's-eye view to see if we could spot any real werewolves.

"I don't see them," I said.

"It's hard when everyone looks like werewolves."

"That's what they were counting on," I said.

As the Ferris wheel started up again, an announcement came over the loudspeaker calling all contestants to the stage to enter the werewolf costume contest.

We all headed over. One by one, the boys filled out the

entry forms and took their places onstage. So did Ryder's crew.

Many people participated. The contestants walked across the stage in front of the howling crowd.

The two judges were local radio celebrities who made notes as they examined the contestants.

After several rounds of eliminations, five contestants were chosen to stand onstage: Ryder, Leopold, Hunter, Nash, and Brandon.

No one knew that four of the five were really werewolves—and the fifth used to be one.

The emcee pulled at Hunter's red beard. "This seems real," he said. "Did you grow this just for the contest?"

The crowd laughed.

"Yes," Hunter said. "And the fangs, too." He grinned, flashing his wolf fangs. The emcee stepped back.

"Wow—those look real. I think there's a wolf out there tonight that is missing some teeth."

The crowd laughed again.

"The four runners-up will win fifty dollars each," the emcee continued. "And our grand-prize winner will take home one hundred.

"And now, for our grand-prize winner, the Legend's Run werewolf for the evening goes to . . . Nash Hamilton!"

Ivy, Abby, Jake, and Dylan cheered with delight at Nash's victory. I couldn't believe the irony. Nash was the winner? The only one who wasn't a werewolf? I had to crack up inside. It was really so odd that the real werewolves weren't recognized as such. And it appeared Nash was really excited by his victory, as he threw his hands in the air, while Leopold and Hunter seemed disappointed and scoffed as they left the stage. I watched Ryder glare at Brandon as they walked backstage. Within a moment, the real werewolves disappeared.

Brandon eventually found us standing in the waiting area. When Nash joined us, Ivy and Abby congratulated him on his prize.

"Where is Ryder?" I asked.

"I don't know. He slipped out," Nash said.

"That means he could be anywhere." I was concerned.

"I know." Nash shook his head in frustration. "I should have kept my eye on him."

"We're going to the candy stand," Ivy said.

"And we're going to the movie," Abby said. "We can all meet up in fifteen minutes."

"No," I said, "we have to stay together."

But my friends and their boyfriends were already heading off in separate directions.

"What do we do now?" I asked Brandon.

He looked around as if he was longing to have fun like everyone else.

"We should be able to enjoy this," I told him. "But instead . . ."

"Well, why can't we? As long as you are next to me, nothing can happen to you."

He grabbed my hand tightly.

"Let's at least enjoy some of the fest," he said.

He led me to the games while I glanced around, thinking at any moment Ryder would be stalking me.

Brandon and I played some of the games and soon we were lost in our own world, laughing, talking, and winning a prize.

"Pick one out from the top row," the carnival operator said to Brandon.

"It's for you," he told me. "Pick out whichever one you want."

Stuffed bears in every color lined the wall. "I'd like that one," I said, pointing to a cute pink one.

The carnival operator pulled the teddy down and handed it to me. I squeezed it with all my might, then gave my handsome boyfriend a squeeze, too.

"I love it," I said.

When we released our embrace, I turned around and bumped into someone.

"Excuse me," I said.

"Excuse me." The voice was deep and calm. I looked up. It was Ryder.

He took my hand. "I was hoping I would bump into you tonight." His wolf fangs caught the moonlight.

I pulled back my hand, but he didn't let go. Ryder's short, spiky hair was long and wavy. He had a thin layer of dark facial hair, and his eyes were intensely gray.

I was afraid he was going to try to bite me.

"Hey—" Brandon said, moving toward Ryder. "Let her go."

Ryder caressed my hand before releasing it. "I guess no one believes we are werewolves," he said.

I backed away, and Brandon stood between us.

"I saw your friends earlier," Ryder said. "We are going to meet up later. Maybe you can join us, too. I was hoping we could all be one happy family."

"My friends wouldn't meet you," I shot back. "Are you crazy?"

"Like a fox. Or should I say wolf?"

"We can end this conversation now," Brandon said.

"You'd like to pay me back for what I did at the championship game?" Ryder asked. "In front of all these people? Go ahead." He put his arms out as if he was going to let Brandon hit him. "Give me your best shot."

"I'm not talking about the past. I'm talking about you leaving her alone."

"That's not going to happen," Ryder said.

Just then we heard screaming, and this time it wasn't coming from the roller coaster. It was coming from behind us. Immediately people were dashing for cover.

I turned back and saw several sets of gray eyes at about the height of a dog. Then I noticed their shiny white coats.

"Wolves!" people yelled. "There are real wolves!"

Couples and children raced for shelter. I froze as the pack

of wolves walked toward us. When they reached us, they stood around Brandon as if he were the leader of their pack.

Ryder stared at Brandon and the wolves in shock.

"What are you, some freak?" he asked.

"Yes, I am," Brandon said.

The wolves began to growl at Ryder.

"I told you to leave my friends alone," Brandon warned.

"They are hanging out with that guy—" I heard someone say.

"Maybe they are his."

"Those are wild animals," another said.

"It could be a trick. Maybe he's their trainer," a male's voice said.

"What's going on?" Ivy asked as she and Abby walked up to us.

I stared at my friends and then looked back at Ryder.

"There's something not right about you," Ryder said to Brandon. "Call off those animals."

"I need a reason to."

"My bite is worse," Ryder said, flashing his fangs.

"I wouldn't count on it." Brandon flashed his fangs back.

Ryder shook his head in disbelief. "It can't be—" he said.

"It can," Brandon told him. "And no one will be the wiser," he said. "It's a perfect night for this. Everyone will think it's part of an act. That was *my* plan."

The wolves growled again.

"Call them off," Ryder said.

Nash appeared. He paused when he saw the wolves and Ryder.

"He's a werewolf, too!" Ryder said. "The judges even thought so."

Suddenly Nash straightened up confidently. It was as if Ryder's words gave him the strength he needed to step up to the situation.

Nash bravely moved to stand next to Brandon.

"Yes," Nash said, "and what are you going to do about it?"

Ryder seemed to quake in the presence of Brandon, Nash, and the wolves.

The crowd of onlookers grew curious as security was now on the scene.

Ryder glared at me—first with fierceness, then at the last moment with a lonely and vulnerable look.

He took off, and within a few seconds Brandon whistled and the wolves howled. Then they ran into the woods.

Brandon slapped Nash on the back. Several people started clapping, and many others joined in.

"Wow—that was cool," one said. "I've never seen wolves up close."

"They were wild—but they seemed as tame as our dog," another commented.

"Well, that was so freaky," Ivy said. "I'm getting tired of wild animals hanging out with us."

"You meant the wolves or that Ryder guy?" Abby said with a laugh.

"I can assure you they are gone for the night," Brandon said. "All of them."

Nash beamed and proudly bumped fists with Brandon.

"Now, how about winning you girls some more prizes at the game area?" Brandon said.

We all wandered over to the booths filled with stuffed animals for those who could puncture a balloon with a dart, knock over a pyramid of milk bottles with a baseball, or toss a ring over the neck of a liter bottle.

We girls smiled as we left the fest with stuffed animals in our hands and hugged good-bye after our eventful evening.

Brandon followed me home in his car and came into my house, making sure I was safe and settled in.

"Well, we foiled their big plan," I said when we sat on the couch in the living room.

"With Nash's help," Brandon added.

We started to watch *Night of the Werewolf*.

"I think I've had enough werewolves for one evening," I said, taking out the DVD and switching to a romantic comedy.

Brandon stroked my hair as I leaned against him and started to doze off.

When I awoke, he was gone and I was holding a stuffed bear instead of him.

SIXTEEN

moonlight meeting

The following day, I found a note laying on our front stoop. On the outside of the folded white paper was typed in black, bold letters, *Celeste*.

I opened the note and read:

Ryder and brood left town. Meet me at dusk at the foot of Morrow Bridge to celebrate.

I texted Brandon:

I'm on my way.

The Morrow Bridge was only a few miles from where I lived. My mom had the car, so I took my bike. I headed down my street and out of our community. I walked my bike across the two-lane street and then pushed it between a barrier and overgrown brush to the gravel pit. I raced around the gravel pit to the bike trail. Once on the bike trail, I pedaled north, noticing the Little River that ran alongside me. My surroundings were so beautiful, and I couldn't wait to meet Brandon. I finally raced over a rusty bridge and stopped at the foot of it. I didn't see my boyfriend anywhere.

I waited for a few moments as the sun set and the full moon shone.

Then I heard Sinatra singing, "Fly Me to the Moon."

I quickly picked it up.

"Where are you?" Brandon asked.

"At the foot of the Morrow Bridge. Just like you asked."

He paused. "I didn't ask you to meet me there," he said.

"I don't understand. You put the note in my mailbox."

"I didn't leave you any note," Brandon said. "I'm waiting for you at my house."

I froze. "Then who am I meeting?" I asked, my voice shaking.

Ryder, in werewolf form, stepped out from behind a dilapidated shack a few yards away.

"I was hoping you'd come," he said seductively.

Ryder was hot—no doubt about it. His jagged black hair was fiercely untamed and fell over his defined shoulders. His arms were beefy, and his tattoos stretched out in monstrous forms. His earrings popped out from underneath his long locks like spikes.

I stood, immobilized. I couldn't breathe. It was like the first time I was lost in the woods, looking into the gray eyes of a hungry pack of wolves. I didn't have Brandon, Nash, my friends, or even a festival crowd to hide behind or give me comfort. My pulse skyrocketed, and I knew I'd have to run for my life.

I turned to escape and head back on the bridge, but I stopped in my tracks. Leopold was waiting on the other side. He appeared menacing as well. His stance was bold and threatening.

"Please help me," I said into the phone. "Ryder and his pack are here. I don't feel safe."

"I'm on my way," Brandon said.

I hung up and slid the phone into my pocket.

I spun around and hopped on my bike. I began to head to the right of where Ryder was standing. But when I pedaled to what I thought was woods, I saw rushing water between the trees. I should have known. There was the river.

I looked back at him.

"I need you, Celeste." His voice was smooth, but I sensed he was cold and calculating.

"No you don't," I reassured him.

"Yes I do. I don't want to be alone forever." His wolf fangs glistened as he spoke.

"Who says that will happen to you? Just because you don't have a girlfriend now . . ."

"But I'm not going to change—I mean, my condition . . . This is who I am. And what girl in their right mind would fall in love with a werewolf?"

I paused. He knew that I loved Brandon, and now he knew Brandon was a werewolf, too.

"That's why you are the perfect girl for me." He gazed at

me with sorrowful eyes. I felt so much intensity coming from him. I felt dizzy.

He pulled me in to him and before I knew it I was on the other end of his lips. He was magnetic and his fingers slid softly through my hair. For a moment, I felt as if I were kissing Brandon. But then I caught a glimpse of his black locks and was shocked back into reality. I realized that this wasn't my boyfriend, and I pushed myself away. I wiped off my lips and spat.

"Why did you do that?" I asked, horrified.

"Because I've been searching for you—" He grinned a wolflike grin.

"Forget it. You'll have to find someone else."

"No, it's you. You are everything I'm looking for. Beautiful, sweet, kind, feisty. Those are all the traits that I want in someone. And I need someone to be with. We all do. Someone like me—and you are that girl."

It was nice to hear those compliments, even from someone as reckless as Ryder. But I wasn't about to get caught up in his seduction again. "I'm nothing like you. You're rude. Pathetic."

"Oh, Celeste, I was just acting. You think I'm really rude? I'm a gentleman."

"A gentleman wouldn't trick a girl into meeting him or into becoming a werewolf."

"I wanted to get to know you. Perhaps I went about it the wrong way. But we are here now, and the moonlight is so beautiful."

"There is nothing beautiful about tonight," I said.

He snarled.

"I'm sure there is a girl for you, Ryder. Someone who will love you. But you can't force someone the way you're trying with me."

"No one will love me the way that I am. I'm a monster—don't you see? So are my friends. What chance do we have? I need someone like you." Ryder was as genuine as I'd ever seen him. Yet I wasn't sure why he was interested in me.

"I don't know what you mean."

"You are so compassionate and understanding. I need a girl like you. Someone who can take care of me—like I take care of her."

"You can't take care of anyone when you scare someone," I said. "Just be yourself. But be a kinder self. You made enemies with Brandon, and you've frightened me and my friends. If you want someone kind, then you have to show up and be kind, too."

His friends crept over and surrounded us.

Ryder came toward me again. He was dangerous and wild. His wolf fangs gleamed near me. There was no escape. I was inches away from being bitten.

I held out my arm to block him. I knew I'd kick him if I had to. But then I thought my words might be more of a deterrent.

"I know how to help you," I said. "And this isn't the way."

"I'm sure you do," he said, not understanding me.

"I have a cure. That's what you really want, Ryder. Not to be with me—but to be yourself. Your*selves*, all of you."

"What kind of cure?" Leopold asked.

Hunter's steely gray eyes brightened. "You can get us a cure?"

"She's lying!" Ryder shouted, grabbing my arm and pulling me away from them.

"What if she isn't?" Hunter asked.

"Yes," Leopold said.

"She has to be. If she had a cure, why wouldn't Brandon have taken it?" he asked.

"Because he gave his dose to Nash," I said, "so *he* could be cured. And it worked for Nash!"

"Who is Nash?" Hunter asked.

"That guy who won the werewolf contest last night at the fest. He used to be a werewolf."

Ryder squeezed my arm tightly.

"You're hurting me!" I shouted.

"Don't—" Leopold said. "She can help us!"

"Yes, let her go!" Hunter insisted.

"I don't care if you are a werewolf," I said. "I'll defend myself if I have to."

"You can't touch me," Ryder growled.

"I can if I have a cure that you never get. I can make sure that you'll be like this forever." Ryder didn't budge.

"I'll give it to *you*, Leopold," I said. "All you have to do is help free me."

"You better let her go, Ryder." Leopold stepped in close, flashing his fangs at his friend.

"Yes," Hunter added. "I don't want to stay like this

forever just so you can have a girlfriend."

All at once a fierce howl came from within the woods behind us. A pack of wolves rushed out and headed straight for us. I covered my face out of fear, then realized they were barking at Ryder and his gang.

Ryder let go of me and growled at the wolves, but they didn't retreat. He stared at them and flashed his fangs, but nothing he did worked to calm them down. They were ready to attack.

I felt a rush of air pass by me, and all of sudden Brandon had pushed Ryder away from me and pulled me out of harm's way. I was so relieved to have Brandon here, I hugged him with all my might.

"Are you okay?" he asked.

I nodded, so grateful my heroic boyfriend was holding me.

The wolves continued to growl at Ryder.

"Call them off," he said.

Brandon got in Ryder's face. "You are a menace as a were-wolf and a human. There is no separation between monster and man except those fangs."

Ryder seemed truly hurt by Brandon's comments. I guessed that was what Ryder feared—that he really was unlovable.

"But it's not the way you look now," Brandon went on. "It's the way you act—always."

Ryder's hurt morphed into anger. His gray eyes grew red with rage.

"You don't know anything about me—" Ryder said.

"You know I do," Brandon challenged back.

"I beat you before, and I can do it again—"

"Not this time," Brandon said.

The wolves crept closer and snarled as if they were ready to kill.

"You need your dogs to do your dirty work," Ryder jabbed.

"And you need a hockey stick to fight dirty," he said, referring to the championship game when Ryder had attacked him. "And now a gang of werewolves to get you a date. I'm not worried."

Brandon whistled, and the wolves retreated. He stepped closer to Ryder. "Now what are you going to do?"

Ryder looked to his friends, but they didn't budge. Instead, they backed off and stepped away from us.

"She said something about a cure—" Leopold said.

"Yes," Hunter said.

"Quit whining," Ryder said, "and help me."

"But we want her to help us. . . ." Leopold said.

"Forget that, you jerks, jump them!"

But Ryder wasn't able to command his pack as easily as Brandon was his.

"It was something she said—" Leopold appeared saddened that what I told him might not be true.

"We were hoping. . . ." Hunter added.

"It's true," Brandon said to them.

They both perked up. "Are you kidding? You have

something to make us human again? All the time?"

He nodded.

They stepped between Ryder and Brandon.

"Hey—" Ryder said. "What are you doing?"

"Exactly what we should have done before," Leopold said. "Finding a new pack leader."

Hunter held Ryder at bay.

"I have to tell you, there's a chance the cure can backfire," Brandon said sincerely, "and you could end up a werewolf full-time."

"It's a chance I have to take," Leopold said.

"Me, too!" Hunter demanded.

"What do I do?" Leopold asked hurriedly.

The two eager werewolves hovered around Brandon as he grabbed the vial from out of his pocket.

"I only have one vial," Brandon said. "But the dose is strong."

"We'll share?" Leopold asked.

Brandon nodded. Then he uncorked the vial and handed it to Leopold.

I admired my boyfriend, who was so gracious to give his cure over to his enemies for the chance of making them well.

Leopold took a sip and handed the vial back to Brandon. Nothing happened.

"I'm going to be like this forever?" Leopold asked nervously. He grew so upset he balled up his fists in frustration. I feared he was going to take off into the woods in despair.

"It's okay," I reassured him. "It takes some time."

"Like how long?" he asked worriedly. "What will happen?"

"You just have to be patient," I said.

"You are just fooling me—maybe what you gave me was poison!"

He began to lunge toward Brandon, but Brandon stepped back before Leopold made contact.

"Just relax," I said to Leopold. I went to him, and his gray eyes tensed in surprise that I'd approached him. I took his hand. He suddenly mellowed. "It's okay," I said. "We are here with you. You aren't alone. It takes a few minutes to affect your body. But we won't leave your side."

Leopold softened; I could feel his tense hand relax.

Then the hairs on his chest began to disappear. One by one. And his beard became shorter and then was gone. His fangs receded and his steely gray eyes turned hazel.

"It worked!" he said, laughing with relief. "It worked!"

"Let me have it," Hunter exclaimed. "It's my turn."

Brandon handed him the vial, and he took a sip.

Hunter tried to remain calm. But he kept checking his chest and arms to see if any hair disappeared.

"It takes time," Leopold assured him.

"I know, I know." He breathed in deeply to calm himself. "But it feels like a lifetime."

"This is all your fault," Leopold said to Ryder. "If you hadn't asked us to sneak into that wolf sanctuary, none of this would have happened."

"Don't blame me—" Ryder said. He was standing a few feet away from us, watching what was transpiring with his friends.

"I do blame you," Hunter said. "If this doesn't work, you'll be the one who needs a sanctuary." Hunter snarled at his former friend as the hairs began to fall off his chest and arms and his biceps returned to their normal size. He flashed a toothy smile and high-fived Leopold.

"Thank you," Hunter said to Brandon as he handed back the vial. "I owe my life to you, man." He shook Brandon's hand and hugged him, like they were players on the ice after a game. Leopold did the same as they were taken with delight in their sudden normalcy.

There was only one sip left. I could see in Ryder's eyes how he craved to take it.

But there was also Brandon, who had been waiting so long to be cured himself.

I didn't know what would happen next. I turned to Brandon, hoping he'd take it, but he didn't move. Instead, he stared empathetically at his last foe.

Brandon extended the vial to Ryder.

Ryder paused for a moment. He looked at Brandon, who was handing him an olive branch.

"I can't believe you'd give me your last dose," Ryder said. "After all we've been through—"

Brandon half smiled. "Go on already."

I, too, felt touched by the magnitude of the situation. Everyone was going to have a chance to be cured—everyone but Brandon. At this point, he was going to remain a were-wolf.

Ryder appeared relieved by the vial of serum and all that it could offer him. He examined it and looked around at all of us. He held it up to make a toast. "Here's to normality." Then he took the last sip.

Nothing happened.

"It's okay," I said. "You have to wait."

But when two minutes turned into three, then four, then five, we all were saddened.

"It's all right—don't panic," Brandon said. "I can call my dad. He can work on another serum."

Ryder was so furious, he let out a ferocious howl. He hadn't been cured. He took off into the woods as we all stood still, saddened by his fate.

"I know he can be cured, too," Brandon said. "If only he would wait."

Hunter and Leopold walked over the bridge with us.

"You were right," Leopold said. "That angry werewolf is who Ryder has always been, even by daylight. Now he just has longer hair."

SEVENTEEN

full moon kiss

For the next month, everything was back to normal—as normal as it could be for a girl who was dating a guy from the Westside who was also a werewolf. Nash continued to be the star athlete in our school and never failed to try to tempt me to rekindle our relationship when he found an opportunity, while Ivy and Abby continued to plan their futures with Dylan and Jake. We three girls were still as close as we always were, talking about guys, love, and the latest fashions. And Brandon and I snuck kisses in between classes and explored the outdoors together after school.

As the next full moon approached, Brandon received a new vial of serum from his scientist father, who had come for a visit.

"This is your vial," Dr. Maddox said, placing it in his

son's hand. "It's not for your friends. Or someone you might happen to meet in the next few days. It's not to be shared or given away. I made it for you. It's *your* cure. So *you* can be normal again."

"I'm not sure I can ever be normal again after everything that has happened," Brandon said.

"These events have made your life richer, that's for sure," his father said. "But you have so many things to look forward to—and I want you to be able to do them as yourself. Not some creature that has to hide in the woods."

"He's really not a creature—not like you'd think," I said. "He's as kind as a werewolf as he is as a human. That's why he shared it instead of taking it."

Dr. Maddox tapped my shoulder. "I'm glad Brandon has you by his side. He's so lucky he found you. This move was good for him after all, even after everything else he's endured.

"I'd stay and watch you take it this time," he said, "but I have to return to Geneva before the moon hits its full appearance. However, this will be my last trip—I'm making arrangements to stay here for good. It will be wonderful to have everything back to the way it was. Only instead of being in Miller's Glen, we'll be here."

I wondered what it would be like if Brandon had the side effects Ryder had and became a werewolf full-time. What kind of life would we have? He wouldn't be able to go to school, and we'd miss spending our days together. If others found out about him being a werewolf, he'd be forced to live in isolation. He couldn't play hockey, hang out with others, or go to college. What kind of future would it be? I only hoped that he was cured like Nash and Ryder's crew. Then he could be human again—but I knew there would be a part of me that would miss those nocturnal moonlit kisses.

On the first night of the next full moon, it was finally Brandon's turn to take the serum. I was as afraid for him as I had been for Nash and as much as I had been the first time I saw Brandon turn. Now he could possibly turn every night and begin an eternal battle within himself that he wouldn't be able to control. But then there was the other side—I was afraid that I'd be losing the side of him that I'd grown to love just as much. In fact, that was who Brandon was to me: a generous, courageous, thoughtful guy in class and a handsome, hot, heroic creature of the night. Could he be one without the other? For his sake, I hoped so, but I had to admit, I'd always miss that side that I'd fallen in love with as well.

After sunset I found him standing up at the tree where I'd seen him first turn. He was gorgeous in his werewolf form, his hair wildly long, his face dotted with manly hair, his chest strong and lean. He was holding the serum, staring at the antidote. He held his fate in his hands.

"Are you ready?" I asked.

"I'm not so sure," he lamented.

"It's okay," I reassured him. "I'm confident it will work like it did for Nash—and Leopold and Hunter."

"That's what I'm worried about."

"I'm not sure I understand."

"The thought of being a werewolf every night terrifies me," he said, fixated on the vial, "and the idea of never being one again makes me sad."

"Really?" I asked. "I feel the same way."

"You do?"

I nodded. "I like you both ways."

He was obviously touched and drew back my hair from my face.

"You are truly special. My dad was right—I am so lucky to have found you."

We embraced as if we were holding on to all the parts of ourselves that we'd come to know.

"So what are you going to do? Aren't you afraid of transforming again?"

"I was when it first happened. But then—I had so much power, being able to explore nature as I never can as a human."

He turned to me with sad and lonely eyes. I could see him struggling to decide who he really was now. Just as I had struggled, too, in preparing to give up some of the parts of him I loved.

"I'm not ready to give up who I am, what I can be, and how I feel once in a full moon."

I nodded my head. Truthfully it would be hard—three days out of the month hiding him away, being isolated or having to avoid making plans with friends. There would be challenges. But wasn't that what life was about anyway?

"I wouldn't want you any other way," I said genuinely.

Brandon held the serum for a moment, then chucked it with all his might far into the woods.

He drew me to him, his lycan fangs catching the moonlight. He leaned in and kissed me long and with such intensity I thought I might explode. He pulled me in to him with a powerful embrace; I didn't want to be anywhere else in the world but in his arms.

I was going to be dating a werewolf for now and for the future. I didn't know what would happen the next day, but I knew it would be exciting. And we'd always be destined for a romantic adventure every so often. . . .

Or at least once in a full moon.

Acknowledgments

I'd like to thank the following fangtastic people for their professional guidance:

Katherine Tegen
Ellen Levine
Sarah Shumway

and for their support, family, and friendship—Jerry, Hatsy, Hank, Wendy, Emily, and Max Lerer, and Linda and Indigo.